W9-BJE-049

WHISPERS OF THE STONES

A High Country Mystery

WHISPERS OF
THE STONES

•

Loretta Jackson and
Vickie Britton

AVALON BOOKS
NEW YORK

Published by Avalon Books,
an imprint of Thomas Bouregy & Co., Inc.
New York, NY

Library of Congress Cataloging-in-Publication Data

Jackson, Loretta.
   Whispers of the stones : a high country mystery / Loretta
Jackson And Vickie Britton.
        p.   cm.
   ISBN 978-0-8034-7474-1 (hardcover : acid-free paper)
1. Murder—Investigation—Fiction.   2. Wyoming—
Fiction.   I. Britton, Vickie.   II. Title.
   PS3560.A224W47 2012
   813'.54—dc23

                                        2011039999

PRINTED IN THE UNITED STATES OF AMERICA
ON ACID-FREE PAPER
BY RR DONNELLEY, HARRISONBURG, VIRGINIA

For two talented Wyoming authors,
Beth Wilkinson and Sandra Guzzo

With special thanks to Dr. George Gill,
whose courses in forensics explore so many
fascinating Wyoming legends

Author's Note

The discovery and subsequent disappearance of the Pedro Mummy is based on a real event in Wyoming history. In the 1930s a tiny mummy was discovered in a cave by miners near Shirley Basin. The wizened little man, seated cross-legged on a ledge, was only fourteen inches tall. The Pedro Mummy became an object of curiosity and scientific speculation until its disappearance in the 1950s. The facts concerning the mummy in this story are true; the rest, of course, is fiction.

Chapter One

Seventy-five-year-old Bill Garr, nicknamed Bartering Bill, lay facedown in the old shed amid a lifetime collection of junk, antiques, and curios. With his dicey heart, everyone had expected to soon hear news of his death, but from natural causes, not from a swift, vicious blow to the back of his head.

Sheriff Jeff McQuede could see no evidence of a struggle. Either the assailant had been lying in wait for him, concealed behind one of the towering old cabinets, or Garr had made the mistake of turning his back to him. As he was struck down, Garr had collided with the worktable. One of the kerosene lamps had fallen, oil mingling with broken glass.

McQuede glanced from the ruined lamp back to Bill Garr's nephew, unprepared for the way the light from the naked bulb overhead had altered him. When Cory Coleman had met him in the yard, and as they had crossed the weedy grounds to the sagging old building, he had looked sick and stunned. His long, hollowed features now seemed ominous, appearing almost to glow with some evil triumph.

"I'm going to ask you to look around," McQuede said. "Let me know if you notice any missing items."

"With all this rubbish, who could tell?" Cory replied.

McQuede noted a different pitch to his voice, supercharged, much too high. Grief often caused a rush of adrenaline, and, for that matter, so did guilt.

"Everything in here is dilapidated." Cory irritably waved a hand around the cluttered room. "It'll take me the rest of my life to rid myself of all this trash."

A strange concern for the moment, McQuede thought.

"Absolutely nothing's fit to sell." Cory, for emphasis, reached out for a violin with a cracked case and broken strings.

"Don't touch anything. Not until my men arrive."

"If you intend to fingerprint this mess, you'd better plan on staying until winter sets in."

McQuede followed Cory's gaze. Every conceivable space was piled high with boxes, stacked on the floor, on display cases with glass half-obscured by grime. A picture of Washington, the kind that used to hang in schoolhouses years ago, hung high on the right wall. Beneath it were framed arrowheads, and below that propped what looked like a battered African death mask.

McQuede turned back to Cory Coleman, the heir apparent to all this and to so much more—all those rolling acres of land that stretched for endless miles toward the Black Mountains.

"Whoever killed him didn't know I was here," Cory announced. "They thought he'd be alone."

"Where do you come from?" McQuede asked.

"Near Sioux City, Iowa. I dropped everything the minute I heard Uncle Bill was so sick. I expected him to die soon—but in his own bed. Not like this!"

"You're on leave from your job?"

"No, I just up and quit. Wasn't in love with it, anyway."

"What do you do?"

"I was working as a consultant. Geology. Nothing I can't live without, but I can go back to it whenever and if ever I want to. Anyway, like I said before, the sneak who killed him would have been scared if they'd known Uncle Bill wasn't alone out here."

"Bill never was alone." The voice from the doorway startled McQuede.

"This is Lex Wisken," Cory explained, casting barely a glance at the newcomer, who had the strong features of a Shoshone. "Bill's hired hand."

"Bill's friend," Lex Wisken corrected, returning Cory's glare. It was obvious no love was lost between them. "The best friend he ever had. Never a day went by that I didn't check on him."

The big Shoshone, whose thick hair hung loose beneath a worn Stetson, stepped into the room. His heavy face, pitted and scarred, made him look even more formidable, enough to stave off a whole gang of thieves single-handedly.

"I thought I was getting away from the crime-infested cities." Cory shook his head. "Hard to imagine robbers way out here in no-man's-land. Uncle Bill should have just let them have whatever they wanted. Maybe they did help themselves. Since he was always adding new merchandise, there's no way of knowing whether anything's missing or not."

Lex began roaming silently around the shed. He stopped before a display case along the left wall and said halfway under his breath, "There is something missing."

"What?" McQuede asked, surprised that anyone could make that assertion faced with this strange jumble of merchandise.

Dim light fell across Lex's blunt features. "The Little Person," he said flatly. "I watched Bill set it in this case. I think it was Friday."

A flash of recognition lit Cory's eyes. "Darned if you're not right! Pedro's gone."

"'Little person'? 'Pedro'? What are you two talking about?"

"Pedro's a mummy," Lex said, once again under his breath.

"About twenty years ago," Cory broke in, "my uncle told me he purchased a strange item, a little mummy, from a dealer up in Casper. He believed it was the Pedro Mountain Mummy. He always boasted about owning it. It gave him some kind of perverse pleasure to know everyone was looking for this mummy, and he was the one who owned it."

McQuede had heard a little bit about this local legend. He knew that a long time ago, maybe in the 1930s, a tiny mummy had been found in a cave not far from here, a curious object that looked like a man but was only about seventeen inches tall. He knew the Shoshone had legends of the Little People, a vicious, elflike tribe who lived in the hills and canyons and shot poisoned arrows. From what he had read, the discovery had made quite a stir, but the Pedro Mummy disappeared sometime in the 1950s and never resurfaced. McQuede had always suspected the miners who brought it in were playing a prank to get attention and that the mummy could have been just a fake.

"Do you think he decided all of a sudden to sell it?" Cory asked.

Lex Wisken stepped closer to an empty glass case. "I watched him place it right there." He pointed to the empty spot in the center of the display. "That's not where he usually kept it. He never let anyone see it. But he told me he was going to make an exception and let some professor take a look at it." Lex looked around as if frightened by Pedro's disappearance. His gaze shifted nervously around the room and lit on a small wooden container that looked like a child's coffin, but instead of heading toward it, he backed away. "He usually kept it in that box."

McQuede drew forward, stooping beside it. Carefully, using only the edges, he tried to open it but found it locked.

"Cory, do you have the key to this?"

Bill's nephew shrugged.

"Mind if I break the lock?'

"Be my guest."

The wood, old and crumbly, gave way to his first pressure. As McQuede lifted the lid, a musty smell of cloth and old wood wafted up from the empty interior.

"He's gone." The big man shrank even farther away, terror now present in his voice.

"I'll be darned," Cory exclaimed. "Someone stole it!" He stopped short, seeming to reconsider his assessment. "Who would want a grisly thing like that? I told Bill on more than one occasion that he should take it out and give it a proper burial."

The Shoshone emitted a stricken moan. "I talked to Bill too. I warned him time and again. I told him that keeping the Little Person was bad luck. The spirit of Pedro is very much alive. But he wouldn't listen."

"If he had Pedro for a couple of decades," McQuede said, trying to assuage the man's fear, "the curse must sure enough work slowly."

"All these years Bill had kept Pedro hidden away. Pedro didn't care. But then Bill brought him out. He may have decided to sell him for his own profit. That must be it! Pedro became angry. He got vengeance on poor Bill, and then he left."

McQuede stared at him a while, in no way able to believe he was serious. "No mummy I've ever seen," McQuede drawled, "ever went anywhere on his own."

"There are powers," the Shoshone replied with profound sincerity, "that you know nothing about."

Cars jammed the driveway. An ambulance from Durmont waited close to the shed, its doors open to receive Bill Garr's body. McQuede had thought Garr's hired man, Lex Wisken, had gone home, but he stood beside the ambulance clutching his worn Stetson in his big, gnarled hands. At the time of death, everyone should have such a loyal presence, McQuede thought, trying to avoid the man's hard, tragic features, which seemed a sculpture of sorrow itself.

Sympathetically McQuede drew forward and stood beside him.

"I did something I never wanted to do," Lex said emptily. "I let him down."

"Many people think that when they lose someone so suddenly," McQuede replied quietly. "But that doesn't make it true."

"Bill was troubled. I knew it, and I didn't help him."

"Did he tell you what was bothering him?"

Lex remained staring straight ahead.

"Did it concern the mummy and his plans to meet with this professor?"

"No, Bill was happy about that. He was proud that someone important wanted to see the Pedro Mummy."

"But who? Surely he mentioned a name to you." McQuede lapsed into silence, his thoughts on the local Durmont professor and his tireless zest for history. "Could he have been Barry Dawson?"

"Bill didn't tell me his name. The only one he mentioned

when I talked to him last night was Bud Lambert. That fool just wouldn't let him alone. He dogged Bill day and night to sell him this property."

"Was he considering Lambert's offer?"

"Bill wouldn't have sold this place at any price." Lex's sullen eyes fixed upon Cory Coleman, following his uneasy motions as he paced back and forth in front of the house. "But *he* will," Lex said resentfully. "Bill always lived in harmony with the spirits, but now the peace has been broken. His death is the start of something evil. I can feel it. It's a darkness that will spread over the land Bill loved so much."

His attention turned to the shed, to the voices inside that had become more distinct. Lex watched solemnly as the paramedics appeared with the gurney, a black zippered bag covering the body.

Lex stood rigidly straight. The dead man's nephew, who had stopped short, now turned away as if to avoid the sight. McQuede's gaze rose to the weathered words above the door, the huge, amateurish letters that slanted downward, BARTERING BILL'S ANTIQUES AND COLLECTIBLES. Remorse settled over him. He recalled Bartering Bill from the rendezvous, from flea markets, from town parades, his loud voice, his boisterous laugh and shaggy hair. Bill had never harmed anyone. Nothing about him justified his meeting a fate like this.

The square white doors closed with a solemn thud. The ambulance pulled away. McQuede turned to Lex again, but before he could speak, the big Shoshone had stalked away. As Lex passed the house, he stopped and glared for a long time at Cory, then with slow, measured steps, he continued to his old truck, which roared in protest as he backed it up and followed the ambulance out to the highway.

As McQuede approached, Cory said, "Did you see how

that old man looked at me? He's always hated me, but I didn't know before just how much." Cory drew in a deep breath. "I think he's crazy. He'd be my prime suspect if I were you."

"He doesn't appear to have a motive," McQuede said.

"In his mind, he does. He's lived on Bill's land ever since he was a kid. He thought his freeloading was a forever thing. Until he found out otherwise. Bill told him last night of his plans to sell out to Bud Lambert."

One of these men was lying, but which one? "Are you going to complete the sale, or do you plan on staying here?"

Bill's nephew answered with pride, "I'm a city man myself."

Cory Coleman looked different in the bright sunlight. He had the deceivingly ordinary looks McQuede often found in a police lineup. At the moment his nondescript appearance seemed part of some kind of careful disguise.

McQuede studied him, wondering how the neat, almost prissy, young man could ever have sprung from the Garr family roots. He appeared in every way to be his uncle's polar opposite. Bill was a regular town character, not someone readily forgotten. He had opinions on every subject and spoke them at the top of his voice. His unruly hair and rough whiskers put McQuede in mind of the other famous Bills—an image Bill did nothing to discourage. "There was Wild Bill, Buffalo Bill, and now there's Bartering Bill," McQuede remembered hearing on the radio. "Come to me for the best bargains in the country."

McQuede supposed the drama and the grandstanding would have embarrassed a prim, somber boy like Cory Coleman. In fact, he had probably fled to the city to get away from it all, to disassociate. And yet the long, thin face and hollow cheekbones gave him away—in the daylight McQuede would have recognized him as Bill Garr's kin anywhere.

"I need to ask you a few more questions," McQuede said.

Cory didn't answer right away but finally replied with resignation, "Let's go inside."

McQuede entered a large, disorderly room, a bachelor's quarters. Full ashtrays, empty bottles, and dirty dishes were strewn about, and clothes hung across chair backs.

Photos were pinned on the wall, mostly of Bill Garr or Garr and Lex Wisken. Missing were pictures of Cory Coleman.

"You and your uncle, were you very close?"

"I spent a lot of summers here," he returned.

Not really an answer, McQuede noted.

"My uncle had no children. He always wanted me to join him in the business."

"But you had other plans." McQuede thought of Bill Garr's failing health, of how anxious he must have been to pass the torch to a person willing, after he was gone, to carry on the work he had loved so much.

"I just never could get interested in antiques and collectibles. They look like so much junk to me."

"Like it or not," McQuede said, "it all belongs to you now."

"Tell me," Cory shot back contemptuously, "who would want to be heir to"—he waved an arm—"this?"

Cory had to have some idea of the value of the property he had just inherited. "Speculators would scramble for the chance," McQuede drawled. "This vast acreage claims mile after mile of prime building lots. It's situated in a top location, right on the highway."

McQuede turned from a photo of Bill in buckskin and faced him. The room smelled of coffee. He wished Cory would offer him a cup, but he didn't.

He simply said, "What do you want to know?"

"The exact date you arrived here."

"Day before yesterday. The doctor wanted Uncle Bill to go into surgery, but he didn't want to. Doc said it was a must. He called me, insisting that I talk him into it. As if that were possible."

"When was the last time you spoke to your uncle?"

"Early this morning Uncle Bill and I had breakfast." As he spoke, his gaze wandered toward the kitchen, to the stack of unwashed dishes in the sink.

"Was he in good spirits?"

"He was seriously ill. When I first got here, I had expected to find him in bed, but he was out and around, sprinting all over the place. He wasn't about to be stopped even if it killed him."

The words "killed him" hung heavily in the air. McQuede finally broke the silence. "Did he have any enemies that you know of?"

"He probably pulled some deals that wouldn't have gone down so well with some of his customers." Cory shrugged. "But I don't think they'd be anything to inspire murder."

"This looks like a crime that occurred on impulse," McQuede told him. "Maybe the outcome of a fight."

"I never fought with him, not once."

"What did you do after your uncle left the house this morning?"

"I'm used to making myself at home here. Bill always went about his normal business. About nine he headed out to the shed." Cory hesitated a moment, then added, "I was tired from my long drive from Iowa and took a little rest. I thought I heard a vehicle pull up a short time later. I didn't look out or think much about it. People are always coming and going."

McQuede's men had already checked the tire tracks, but because there were so many, it would be futile attempting to link any of them to the crime. "Did he get any phone calls this morning?"

"As a matter of fact, he did, around nine."

"Any idea who called?"

"No. He left right after that. When he didn't come in for lunch, I went out to check on him. That was probably about one. At first I thought he'd simply collapsed or fainted. Then I saw the blood."

"His phone call suggests that he may have had an appointment."

"I wouldn't know. I didn't hear what they were talking about."

"Do you mind if I take a look around? Your uncle may have left some notes."

"He took the call from the phone in his office," Cory said reluctantly, less eager now to be helpful.

On Bill Garr's desk was an old-model phone with no redial button.

"I'll have to check the phone records," McQuede said.

Cory stood in the doorway, looking suddenly nervous and jittery. McQuede made no point of noticing. He continued to search the desktop and lifted a yellow pad there. A phone number had been scrawled across the top of the scratch pad. Below it the words *appointment 10:30* were circled. McQuede placed the note in his billfold.

Cory ran a hand in agitation through his light brown hair, causing a stubborn cowlick to rise. "Aren't you supposed to have a search warrant?"

"We don't need a warrant to go through the personal effects of a victim."

"His private business doesn't have anything to do with the robbery," Cory said belligerently. "How long do you plan to be rummaging around out here?"

"As long as it takes." McQuede stopped all motion to assess him. It was possible that Cory had come out here expecting to find his uncle dying and was disappointed by the notion that he might have to wait quite a long time to claim his inheritance.

Cory, as if reading his mind, bristled. "I'm not trying to hide anything from you. I want his killer found much more than you do!" His voice, now loud and blustering, caused the resemblance to Bill Garr McQuede had noted earlier to magnify. Perhaps because of this, McQuede found himself hoping the young man wasn't guilty. But right now, as sole heir, he had to be McQuede's prime suspect.

But why the missing mummy? Was that just part of some false scenario the nephew had concocted to throw him off the track?

Cory, exactly the way Bill would have, burst out, "What else do you want from me?"

"Nothing, now," McQuede returned. "If you remember or find out anything that might be pertinent to his death, you give me a call."

As McQuede left the old frame house, his deputy, Sid Carlisle, was striding toward him. Strange, the way his uniform, unlike McQuede's, never looked wrinkled and mussed, and his gray hair always remained neatly smoothed back from his handsome features.

"Bartering Bill's must have been a popular place," Sid told him. "Fingerprints everywhere. Not much chance of sorting out the killer's, even if he had left them."

"How about the front entrance?"

"We lifted prints from the doors, but they probably belong to the nephew who found the body."

"What about the mummy?" McQuede asked.

"He's not inside that shed, I'll guarantee you."

"Any luck locating the murder weapon?"

"Not yet. The coroner said he was struck with a smooth, metal object, like a lamp base or an iron pipe."

"Extend the weapon search to the whole area," McQuede said.

Sid went back inside.

No murder weapon, no fingerprints—zero leads. Only one clue existed for McQuede to follow up on—the mysterious professor who had wanted to view the missing mummy. McQuede didn't know how he'd locate him, but he would start by paying a visit to Barry Dawson.

Chapter Two

In late afternoon McQuede could generally find Barry Dawson in Nate's Trading Post, which was owned by the elderly Shoshone Nate Narcu. McQuede often joined Nate and the professor, the three of them an unlikely trio gathered around the potbellied stove to talk over the day's events.

As McQuede entered the store, Nate said in his soft-spoken way, "I made a fresh pot of coffee, Jeff. Just help yourself."

McQuede took a mug from one of the nails on the wall, filled it, and pulled up a captain's chair between Nate and the professor. Before he sank into it, he caught their images in the mirrored display case set off to the right. He could see only Nate's slightly stooped, flannel-covered back and his own rugged appearance, one that contrasted sharply with Dawson's slender, aristocratic good looks. Unlikely trio, indeed.

McQuede drank deeply of the strong coffee, braced by it and by the crackling fire that offered warmth against the cool autumn day.

Nate leaned forward. His dark, weathered skin made him look ancient, except for those brilliant eyes, so quick to see and understand. "Barry just told me about Bill Garr."

As always, McQuede was surprised at how quickly information spread, how the word of Garr's murder had preceded him into Durmont.

Obviously the news of Garr's death had not affected Barry Dawson as much as it had Nate. He said in an almost humorous manner, "Even the loudest of voices can be silenced."

McQuede, with a censorious glance toward Dawson, stated, "It looks like an attempted burglary gone wrong."

"Better watch your back, Nate. You may be next."

McQuede turned to Dawson. "When was the last time you saw Bill Garr?"

"Hey, don't be looking at me," Dawson joked. "I pay dearly for every artifact I acquire."

"What was stolen would fit in nicely with your Native American collection," McQuede returned. "Do you know anything about Garr's owning a little mummy, one he believed to be the long-missing Pedro Mountain Mummy?"

Dawson removed his rimless glasses and cleaned them with his handkerchief. His previous good humor drained away. "Of course, I was excited when I first heard him boasting about it. I drove right out to Bartering Bill's, but for nothing. Bill flatly refused to even show it to me." As Dawson put the glasses back on, they glinted against the glare from the overhead bulb, light eyes blending with his pale skin and graying hair. His manner became less serious again. "I concluded that the whole story was made up, just another gimmick of Bill's to call attention to himself and to draw people out to that junk pile."

"His hired man, Lex Wisken, says otherwise. He had seen

the mummy recently and was the one who pronounced it missing. It could be a direct tie-in with Bill Garr's murder."

They both stared at McQuede disbelievingly.

"I was wondering what the two of you could tell me about this Pedro Mountain Mummy."

"Don't be thinking Bill Garr had the real Pedro Mummy," Dawson said, "because he probably didn't. The authentic one has quite a history."

"I always heard rumors that the mummy was a fake, one the miners were going to use as a hoax to get money and publicity."

"Oh, no. Let me explain." Dawson's eyes brightened, and he cleared his throat.

McQuede, accustomed to the professor's long lectures, settled back in his chair.

"A couple of prospectors by the names of Cecil Mayne and Frank Carr were digging for gold in 1932 up in Shirley Basin. When they dynamited a cave, they discovered this small, naturally preserved mummy seated cross-legged on a high shelf of rock."

"One of the Little People," Nate broke in. "Like in the Shoshone legends."

"Seated, the little man was only seven inches tall." Dawson raised his hands to indicate the exact length. "Standing he would be about seventeen inches. The curious little mummy had the wizened face of an old man, large, bulbous eyes, and a wide, thin-lipped mouth."

"What became of the mummy?"

"The miners sold it, and it changed hands several times. For a while, it was displayed at the old Jones Drugstore in Meeteetse. In the late forties Jones sold it to a Casper businessman, Ivan Goodman, who showcased the artifact as a sideshow attraction. In the fifties Goodman took the mummy to New York to be examined by scientists. Based on the perfectly formed skeleton and the full set of ribs, scientists estimated it was the remains of a man of about sixty-five years of age at the time of his death. Then, in the seventies, another group of scientists out of curiosity went over the old X-rays and proposed the theory it might not have been a little man after all, but a deformed infant." Dawson shrugged. "So as you can see, throughout the years, there's been much disagreement about the Pedro Mummy."

Bells jingled as the front door opened and closed. A lean, blond man in jeans and cowboy hat entered. Among other dealings, all of them suspect, Frank Larsh, more commonly known as Ruger, had a hand in the collectibles and antiques trade. McQuede knew Ruger would go any length to turn a profit, legally or illegally, although he had never been able to make any charges against him stick. Ruger set a heavy box of wares he hoped to sell to Nate on the counter, which Nate eyed with casual interest.

"Eventually, the mummy disappeared from the public eye," Dawson continued as if Ruger hadn't entered. "It probably fell into the hands of some private collector."

"And now it has supposedly ended up in Bill Garr's shed," McQuede remarked.

"Or so it was rumored."

Ruger, apparently not interested, began arranging his treasures on Nate's counter: a rusty toy bank, a granite coffeepot, an old brass spittoon.

"Regardless, I keep thinking this mummy may have caused Garr's death." McQuede set his empty coffee mug on the old wooden barrel that set nearby. "But I don't understand why. I can see killing over a rare jewel or priceless antique, but what kind of a nutcase would want to make off with a tiny, dried up corpse?"

Ruger, who had been listening after all, swung around. "I would! This isn't just any mummy you're talking about, is it? This is the Pedro Mountain Mummy." He gave a low whistle. "So the rumors the old man had it all these years were true. I tried to buy it off him once, but he wouldn't sell it or even let me see it. I always assumed he was bluffing, that he thought the idea of his having old Pedro stashed away added to his prestige."

"But why would anyone want something like that? You could hardly set a tiny little dead man on the coffee table for a conversation piece."

"But what a draw it would make." Ruger's eyes lit with enthusiasm. "The same people who like to go to carnivals would pay good money to see it!"

McQuede could imagine Ruger with his shocks of longish blond hair dressed up like some circus ringmaster, charging a dollar a head to view the latest sideshow attraction. It wasn't a pretty picture.

"I wouldn't keep it, of course. Sammy knows all kinds of collectors who'd dig deep in their pockets for something like that."

"Congratulations," McQuede drawled, "you've just made my list of suspects." Actually, he wasn't joking. He had long suspected Ruger's part-time antiquing business and isolated ranch home was a front for stolen property that he fenced through his pal Sammy Ratone in Vegas.

Ruger raised his hands in mock protest. "If Bartering Bill was killed this morning, I have an ironclad alibi."

"Don't you always?" McQuede regarded him coldly. "Tell me, Ruger, what price would Sammy Ratone put on this mummy?"

Ruger shrugged. "Who knows? The amount might be without limits."

"The Little Person was human like anyone else," Nate said, shaking his head. "His remains should be respected, should never have been for sale at all."

"Legally, it's not allowed, but unfortunately that doesn't stop under-the-table deals." McQuede glanced back at Dawson, "What else do you know about the mummy's history?"

"According to a 1950 edition of the *Casper Tribune-Herald,* Goodman stated that scientists agreed the mummy was authentic, the 'only specimen known of a human race of that type that perhaps dated back a million years.'"

McQuede marveled at Dawson's grasp of the subject, at his knack for recalling exact details. "But those were Goodman's words," McQuede clarified, "not the scientists."

"I heard the skull had been smashed as if by a heavy blow," Ruger cut in. "Looks like the old boy met a violent end, just like Bartering Bill."

"The first set of scientists may have been wrong." Dawson's brow furrowed. "The later group who reviewed the old X-rays in the seventies believed the mummy might not have been an old man at all as was first believed, but that of a child born with anencephaly."

"Ane—what?" Ruger asked, leaning forward.

"A rare birth defect that causes most of the cranium and brain to fail to develop properly. The portion of the brain that has formed is often exposed, which might explain the appearance of the flattened head. They believed the remains were those of a malformed child who had died and whose parents had placed it in the cave."

"That seems likely," McQuede said.

"I heard he had teeth," Ruger challenged. "What baby is born with a full set of teeth?"

McQuede cast him an annoyed look. It was difficult to talk sense with Ruger chiming in every moment.

"And if it was a deformed child," Ruger added, "why would they bury the body like that? The local tribes, the Arapahoe and the Shoshone, don't bury their dead in caves, do they, Nate?"

Nate shook his head.

"All we can determine from the 1950s X-rays," Dawson said, "is that the ribs shown were decidedly human; however, it is still debated whether the mummy was a deformed child or a full-grown little man. We'll never be certain unless the mummy turns up again and can be reexamined."

"Other theories exist," Nate said. "About the Little People."

"I know what you're talking about, Nate. Some believe the mummy could be the only existing specimen of the Nimerigar, a pygmy race who were mentioned in Shoshone and other Native American legends."

"My grandfather used to tell how the Nimerigar lived in the mountains and the canyons," Nate Narcu said in a quiet, faraway voice. "They built dwellings made of sticks and stones. They were swift runners and attacked the Shoshone with tiny bows that shot poisoned arrows."

So this was the source of Lex Wisken's superstitions.

"They kept to themselves and were seldom seen." The old Shoshone's voice was deep and slow-paced. "Most of them were malicious and played pranks like getting travelers lost and stealing children. They're the ones who made the drawings back in the caverns. The Little People don't like you looking at the stone pictures."

"But not all encounters with the Little People were bad," Dawson explained. "It was also believed if you captured one, it would bring good luck, like a leprechaun or elf."

"Owning a mummy didn't bring Bill Garr much luck," McQuede observed.

Nate spoke again with calm certainty. "It would have, had not the harmony been disturbed."

Lex Wisken had voiced the identical thought. And maybe they weren't so far wrong—the absence of harmony does leave a void open to evil, an evil present in every generation. In addition to this attack on Bill Garr, it looked to McQuede as if a crime might also have occurred years ago. "I guess we'll never know how Pedro met his fate, whether or not he was murdered."

"It was told that the Nimerigar killed their own when they became old or ill," Nate said, "by smashing their skulls."

McQuede thought of the little mummy sitting in his cave with his bashed-in skull, then of the vicious blow Bartering Bill Garr had received. The similarities made him uneasy.

"If these little guys are still hiding out in these mountains," Ruger said tauntingly, "I've sure never seen one."

"You wouldn't," Nate replied, as if Ruger deserved a serious answer. "They would keep to themselves. They wouldn't be seen unless they wanted to be seen. The Little People are thought by most to have died off now, although some of the Shoshone still tell tales of seeing them. Others believe that their spirits still remain in the canyon."

"Lex Wisken can be counted among them," McQuede added with amusement. "Lex went so far as to say that the mummy was the one who had done Garr in."

Ruger laughed loudly. "In that case our famous sheriff is in deep trouble. That little fellow is going to be hard to catch. I can just see McQuede trying to duck those little poisoned arrows!"

McQuede glanced at Dawson, expecting him to supply some joking retort, but it was Nate who spoke.

"Don't make light," he cautioned, "of what you know nothing about."

"I'll have to go along with Ruger. I don't believe in the supernatural." McQuede paused. "Mummies don't kill people. And they don't just get up and walk on their own accord."

"I'm sure Nate was referring to the entire Nimerigar myth," Dawson said supportively. "And he's right—legends are often based on truth. I, for one, don't totally discount the notion that a race of tiny people once roamed this area."

"Explain to me why this mummy, which may or may not be authentic, is so important."

"The Pedro Mummy hasn't been seen for over fifty years. Because DNA and other testing wasn't available then, many scientists would consider even a slim chance like this a great opportunity. You should talk to some of them I know. They live and breathe theories, and modern genetic technologies could provide answers."

"I don't see how this find would prove that the Little People existed."

"Take my word, McQuede, it could be of crucial importance. Tiny bones have been found in other places. In Cochoton, Ohio, and in Coffee County, Tennessee, burial grounds have been discovered containing the remains of dwarflike people."

Dawson's manner could change in midsentence, from dry and dull to zestfully enthusiastic.

"You've surely heard about the remains recently found on the Indonesian island of Flores. They were of a pygmy race about the size of chimpanzees—*Homo floresiensis,* which the scientists nicknamed Hobbits."

Dawson fell silent, one hand raised to his forehead as if to help him think. "If it's not a fake," he stated at last, "that little mummy could be invaluable. Can't you see, McQuede?

It might be the only known specimen of a prehistoric tribe that once roamed this very land!"

"Then many scientists could be willing to go to any length to get their hands on it."

"Yes! What a glorious opportunity. It could be a significant scientific breakthrough. Imagine, finding proof that a tiny race of people believed to be only legend actually existed. Why, it would lead to limitless funding for research."

"And whoever took the credit would gain fame and fortune overnight," McQuede concluded.

As if some surprising thought had just occurred to him, Dawson exclaimed, "McQuede, I know just the person you should talk to. Professor Seth Talbot is in the area now—you know, the man who recently wrote that best-seller about our local petroglyphs, *Whispers of the Stones.* Talbot recently placed an ad in a professional journal and another on the Internet offering fifteen-thousand dollars for any information about the missing Pedro Mummy."

"Which leads me to ask," McQuede broke in, "why a celebrity like Talbot would be hanging around Durmont."

"He's volunteered to assist on that special Native American project sponsored by the Smithsonian. The exhibit, which will open in Denver, includes a study of the nearby Black Mountain's petroglyph caves."

"Do you know where I can find him?"

"I heard he was staying at the Grand View Hotel."

McQuede pulled up to the Grand View Hotel, which rose twelve stories above the flat-roofed businesses that lined the main street—a skyscraper by Durmont's standards. The lobby, lit by crystal chandeliers and adorned with huge paintings of the Black Mountains, made a startling contrast to the blandness outside.

"Where can I find Seth Talbot?" he asked the young clerk.

The kid reacted nervously. "Mr. Talbot wouldn't like it if I gave out his room number."

"I won't like it if you don't."

"He's staying in suite 1204," the boy replied reluctantly.

McQuede took the elevator to the top floor and entered a spacious hallway. He rapped on the door. "Jeff McQuede. I'd like to have a word with you."

"I informed the desk that I didn't want to be disturbed," an arrogant voice called. "I'll be signing autographs tonight at the Pegasus Bookstore at seven."

He thought McQuede had come way up here to get his autograph. What audacity! McQuede drew in his breath. "I'm the sheriff of Coal County. I'm here on important business."

McQuede had expected Seth Talbot to be a carbon copy of Barry Dawson, complete with rimless glasses and immaculate gray suit. He was surprised to find a large, burly man wearing a heavy sweater and sporting an unkempt beard reminiscent of Ernest Hemingway. He looked capable of handling himself, though, perhaps better in a photo shoot than in the rough-and-tumble real world.

McQuede could tell at a glance that impressing people would be his number one concern. Although near McQuede's age, in his early forties, Talbot probably had convinced a lot of giddy students, mostly girls, of his place among the great.

McQuede stepped into the huge room. "I'm investigating the death of Bill Garr."

"And why should that be of interest to me?"

"It looks as if he was murdered in an attempted robbery. Strange, that the only item missing was a little mummy."

In a miffed manner, Talbot swung around and walked to

a round table at the window, where an open laptop computer sat beside a high stack of books. He seated himself and made a point of staring at McQuede, a method used to intimidate. Clearly he was accustomed to squaring off with rivals and was trying to put McQuede on the defensive.

McQuede didn't play that game. He ambled forward and sank into the chair opposite him. "How long have you been in town?"

"I arrived last Monday. Not quite a week. I flew here right after my book signing in New York City."

McQuede glanced out the window, at the small town cut into by railroad tracks, often noisy from the sound of trains, heavy cars laden with coal from the Preston Mine. "Hard for Durmont to compete with New York."

"On that we agree."

"The dead man I'm concerned with ran a place called Bartering Bill's. You ever hear of him?"

"I don't even know him. What I'd like to know is who's been trying to implicate me. Is it Barry Dawson?" He continued staring at McQuede, as if McQuede would back down because of the steely eye contact. "Of course Dawson's behind your being here. He's got a big-time grudge against me."

Talbot, with a smile of satisfaction, glanced away. "My influence blocked him from being a part of the Smithsonian project, a position he wanted very badly."

McQuede made no reply.

Tabot hit his flat hand against the table, causing a reordering of the books. "I want to know just what he told you!"

"No one had to tell me anything. It's common knowledge that you ran an ad offering top money for information on the Pedro Mummy. Is that going to be the title of your next book? *The Pedro Mummy and the Little People*?"

"My work would not be of any interest to either you or your small town."

"Some of us are learning to read," McQuede drawled.

Talbot raised his dark eyebrows mockingly. "Glad to hear it. Send a few of them to my book signing tonight."

As McQuede studied him, he thought of Barry Dawson's vast knowledge, of Nate's wisdom. Talbot would have to borrow from men like them. "Why would you object to Professor Dawson being on the project?"

"He lacks . . ." Talbot stopped midsentence. "I don't have to discuss this with you."

"But you do have to discuss Bill Garr with me."

"Garr got wind of my generous offer for information and contacted me while I was in New York City. By that time I had become very sorry I'd put out that ad. You have no idea how many lunatics there are in this world. And every last one of them must have responded to that advertisement. I'm almost afraid to answer the phone."

"But once you arrived in Durmont, you surely would have gone out to see him."

"I intended to, but I'm a very busy man. Besides, I didn't think there was much of a chance that his so-called find would turn out to be authentic. Truthfully, I even doubted that it existed anywhere except in his head."

"His hired man saw the mummy right before Garr's death. So what could have happened to it?"

"That's easy to answer. He must have already sold it."

"In any event, Garr had an appointment to meet a professor. I thought it might be you."

"Have you asked any other professors? If they knew about this Bargaining Bill or whoever he was actually having a mummy, they would like nothing better than to beat me to it."

"I've talked to Dawson."

"What about Arden Reed? Come to think about it, I told Professor Reed about my plans to check with Bill Garr the first chance I got."

"Reed's the man who's heading the Denver exhibit?" McQuede asked.

"Yes, Dr. Reed is from the Smithsonian. He specializes in Native American studies and has a specific interest in the indigenous peoples' cave drawings. I take it you've read about my discovery of the petroglyph cave in Black Mountain." As Talbot looked at a stack of his book, *Whispers of the Stones*, he gave another self-indulgent smile. "I think Arden Reed begged me to join the project so he could pick my brain about the Little People. He saw what a success I'd made with this book. He probably plans to write one himself."

McQuede doubted his story of having never contacted Bill Garr. Talbot didn't look like a man who would put any opportunity on hold. "So you claim you did not so much as call Bill Garr after arriving here on Monday?"

Irritation crept into Talbot's voice. "How many times am I going to have to answer that? I've never laid eyes on Bill Garr."

"Then I guess I'll need to have a talk with Arden Reed. Do you know where I could find him?"

"That wonderful curator, Loris Conner, has allowed us to set up temporary headquarters at the local museum."

McQuede's heart sank at the mention of Loris' name. They had been dating for several months now, and he certainly didn't want her mixed up in this.

"If you hurry, you might still catch him," Talbot said.

McQuede got to his feet, his gaze locking on the cover of Talbot's book, the crude outline carved in stone of a small hunter aiming a bow and arrow. He laid several bills down on the table. "I'll just buy one of your books while I'm here. Need to catch up on my reading."

With a smile less pretentious this time, Talbot opened a copy of *Whispers of the Stones* and with a flourish scribbled his name—nothing else.

This account of Talbot's discovery of the Black Mountain cave drawings he no doubt planned to tie in with the Little People in a follow-up novel. That was why he was willing to lay down hard cash for information on the Pedro Mummy. A subject like that was bound to stir up great interest regardless of whether the creature turned out to be a malformed infant or one of a small tribe that had wandered the Wyoming mountains. The media would pounce on the news, just as they had on Houdini's magic tricks and on the bits of plates and other artifacts salvaged from the *Titanic*. McQuede did not begin to understand the impact such a discovery as the tiny mummy would have on science, but he did see a possible motive for murder.

Chapter Three

McQuede was driving toward the museum to talk to Arden Reed when he remembered it was Friday—a time of the week he never failed to set aside for his budding romance with Loris Conner. He checked his watch. If he hurried, he could still change clothes and pick her up at seven. McQuede wasn't going to make the mistake with her that he had made with the other women who had paraded through his life, whom he had always placed second to his work. He swung the squad car around and, with foot heavy on the gas pedal, lost no time arriving at his little house at the edge of Durmont.

Just as McQuede pulled into the drive, his cell phone rang. "Jeff, it's Loris." She hesitated. "It's been such a hectic day. We're both so busy, would you care if I canceled to-night?"

"If that's what you want to do."

"I'll call you tomorrow."

Disappointment surged through him. Loris and he had been dating for several months and had already settled into a comfortable routine. They had not missed a single Friday night of dining at that new, fancy steakhouse, Shadow Mountain Inn.

Determination clashed with resignation. He had no intention of spending Friday night without Loris. The sound of her laughter, their long talks, meant too much to him. Loris cared about his work, about whether or not some cold-blooded murderer got away with a crime.

He'd just drop by her office and persuade her to postpone her work as he was intending to do his.

Loris' car wasn't parked in the lot in front of the Coal County Museum, but he found the door of the museum unlocked. He strode by the stuffed black bear, that greeter of visitors, angry paws extended, mouth snarling. He passed the Native American collection with its abundance of pottery, beaded garments, and arrowheads, and paused for a moment by the display Loris had just completed that featured his great-uncle, his namesake, the famous lawman Jeffery McQuede.

He gazed at the black letters underneath: *Wyoming Territory—1874.* Looking at the photo was almost like gazing into a mirror—the same dark hair and silvery eyes, the same resolve.

Aunt Mattie had donated most of the items, the .44 model Winchester rifle, the solid silver badge, the worn holster where tough, old Jeff McQuede had placed his gun. McQuede had inherited the .45, his prize possession.

His image reflected in the glass caused him to run a hand through his unruly hair. He had shaved this morning, but already his chin felt bristly and seemed almost a match for the old lawman's whiskers. McQuede was careful to shave every day, or he would end up looking exactly like him.

When McQuede reached the corridor, he was gripped by another disappointment. The door to Loris's office was closed, and no light showed through the glass pane.

Talbot had mentioned that the Smithsonian crew had set up temporary headquarters at the museum. No doubt they had taken over the area that consisted of a large conference hall and a couple of empty offices. He would probably find her working over there. He hurriedly crossed the museum proper toward a huge room where he found not Loris but a lone woman seated at a laptop computer. Piles of maps and photos were spread out on the table before her.

She turned to him with surprise. Her light brown hair was tied back, drawing attention to her receding chin and to her thin, angular features. Behind her, the computer screen showed a series of photographs of rock carvings similar to the one on Seth Talbot's book cover.

"Are you looking for Dr. Reed?" she asked in a brisk, efficient way. "If so, you just missed him, but he'll be here around seven in the morning."

"Actually, I was looking for Loris."

The woman smiled. "You just missed her too."

McQuede turned away, then back. "Are you from the Smithsonian?"

"No. I'm Terese Deveau, forensic anthropologist. I teach at the lab in Casper."

McQuede was familiar with the lab, where the bones of murder victims were often sent for identification or facial reconstruction.

"Far as I know, no bones were found in that famous cave discovery Talbot made here a couple of years ago," McQuede said, "only rock drawings."

"Which is also within my area of expertise. Dr. Reed invited me to join the project because of my work on the Black

Mountain petroglyphs." Her serious, all-business manner had made her at first seem unattractive, but her rather long, aquiline nose seemed to fit with her high cheekbones and slightly wide mouth. He liked her outdoor look, the tanned skin and amber eyes with the crinkles at the corners.

"Where did you study?"

"At the University of Wyoming. As an undergraduate I worked with Seth Talbot, which accounts for my interest in petroglyphs. Dr. Reed and I met at the convention in Casper, and he insisted that I take a sabbatical and help him with the project."

McQuede suddenly wanted to know more about this job Loris was so enthused about. "Tell me a little about it."

"It's called Rock Art of Wyoming and the Colorado Plateau. We're focusing on the Lost Cave and are building plaster casts showing some of those carvings. That's why Dr. Reed wanted to hire Dr. Talbot."

"What are you working on?"

"Right now I'm finding photographs to use to give a historical background. They will depict the different eras. I wanted Barry Dawson to be in charge of local tribes and their art, but since he wasn't hired, Loris will be doing that. She plans to use push-button recordings so people can listen to the local legends."

McQuede wanted to know more, but it was fast getting late. "I suppose I can catch Loris at home," he said, turning again to the door.

"She left, but she didn't go home. I think you'll find her at the Shadow Mountain Inn."

At first, this surprised him; then he realized that the news of Bill Garr's death had reached her. It was just like Loris to be overly considerate, not to want to interfere in any way with his work, so she must have gone out to what he considered "their place" to dine alone. He'd just stop by there and surprise her.

The locals considered the steakhouse, with Black Mountain hovering in the background, the ultimate in high style. He pulled into the driveway, thinking of Loris seated by herself at their special table near the window, and imagined her joy upon catching sight of him.

To the disconcertion of the headwaiter, McQuede pushed past the PLEASE WAIT TO BE SEATED sign and entered the room. Loris sat with her back to him, thick, honey-blond hair swept up in a fashionable way. His heart sank at the sound of her voice, then her laughter, both directed toward the distinguished-looking man who sat across from her.

McQuede hated the man on sight—despising the tall, rangy look of him, the touches of gray at his temples that exaggerated the blackness of his hair. To top it all off, he reached across the table and caught Loris' hand.

The moment McQuede reached them, the man released his grasp and rose in a gentlemanly fashion.

Loris looked up at him, her hazel eyes widening with surprise. "Jeff," she said quickly. "I want you to meet Arden Reed. Arden and I planned to work late, so I didn't think I'd be able to take time for dinner."

McQuede couldn't quite believe this. He had convinced himself that Loris had cancelled their standing date because of *his* investigation. He hadn't once thought that her concern was because of her own work—or this new man in town.

"Loris"—Arden Reed spoke gallantly—"is fast becoming my right hand. We've accomplished so much today, work I couldn't have completed without her. The least I could do was invite the lady to dinner."

The least, McQuede repeated to himself. At the fanciest restaurant in town, at their restaurant, at their table.

McQuede attempted to keep the hostility from sounding in his voice. "I've been wanting to talk to you, Professor," he said, "about the death of Bill Garr."

"I'm sure this can wait," Loris broke in. "I think we all deserve to enjoy a pleasant meal."

Reed directed a beaming smile at her. "Methinks the lady is always right!"

A stupid attempt at misquoting Shakespeare, McQuede thought. Reed would have no trouble charming the women back east. McQuede gave Loris a sideways glance and extended Reed's domain, even to the wilds of Wyoming.

"I've been trying to talk Loris into coming to Denver to work on our special Native American project," Reed said enthusiastically.

"I'm sure you have," McQuede replied. He glanced toward Loris, but she avoided looking at him. McQuede straightened up. "If you don't mind, I do need some answers from you," he said.

"But not right now. Just sit down here, Jeff. We've ordered the shrimp scampi. I know how much you like seafood."

How could she be so casual about breaking his heart? McQuede did seat himself beside her but waved away the waitress who hovered nearby with a menu. His appetite had completely left him.

McQuede spoke doggedly to Arden Reed. "Did you ever have any contact with or make any phone calls to Bill Garr?"

"Oh, Jeff," Loris said, casting him a censorious look, no doubt resenting his turning her outing with her handsome new boss into an interrogation.

Reed held up a hand. "That's okay, Loris. I can answer that quickly. No, I've never talked to him or met him. Why do you ask?"

"I spoke to Dr. Seth Talbot today. He thought you might have paid Garr a visit. To look at the Pedro Mummy."

Arden Reed answered earnestly and directly, "I wouldn't cut out a fellow worker," he said. "Dr. Talbot planned to check with Mr. Garr, and that was good enough for me."

McQuede tried not to direct at Reed one of those belligerent stares Talbot had given him. Reed wasn't of the same breed as Talbot, wasn't contentious or self-important, apparently not a man who would, as Talbot had claimed, try to snatch the Pedro Mummy story for himself. In fact, McQuede might even have liked Reed had he not been having dinner with the woman he loved.

"What else can you tell me?"

"I was under the impression that Seth Talbot had made an appointment with Garr," Reed volunteered. Then, as if realizing his words might place Talbot in a bad light, he quickly added, "Of course, I don't know whether he followed through with it."

"We have ways of finding out who's telling the truth and who's not." McQuede stated this outright lie in an unnecessarily admonishing tone.

Arden Reed met McQuede's notorious silvery gaze steadily, frankly. "I hope you can. I, for one, have nothing to hide."

Loris had listened, bewildered. "Please, Jeff," she protested.

McQuede rose. "I'll be in touch, Mr. Reed. It may be necessary for you to come down to the station for further questioning."

McQuede's yellow dog, one he had adopted from a crime scene, met him at the door, tail thumping happily. Psy emitted a series of sharp, crazy barks that had earned him his name, short for *Psychotic.*

"At least someone's glad to see me." McQuede stooped to pat the bristly fur.

Psy barked again, then stopped, eying McQuede hopefully, sniffing at the bag that contained the hamburger McQuede had picked up at the fast-food drive-through on his way home.

McQuede sank down in the recliner and began to unwrap the hamburger. The mutt watched with large, watchful eyes.

"I was hoping to have a prettier dinner companion than you tonight," McQuede told him. He took a portion of the hamburger and tossed it into the air. Psy skillfully caught it, gulping it down in one bite.

"And one with more manners," McQuede added.

McQuede couldn't stop thinking about Loris. Was she really considering taking the temporary assignment in Denver? Her leaving, even for a short while, would leave a dark, empty void.

He had gotten too comfortable, had taken their relationship for granted. Because he had no interest in dating others, he had assumed she felt the same way, but evidently he had been wrong.

McQuede felt ashamed of the way he had stormed into the restaurant and had persisted in questioning Reed. Although he had good reason to consider Reed a suspect, he knew his own feelings of jealousy had prompted his not-so-admirable actions.

Reed, on the other hand, had maintained his poise, his charm and refinement. Loris must surely be comparing them, and McQuede must surely be turning out the loser.

He couldn't blame Loris for being drawn to Reed. After all, he was highly successful and sophisticated, a far cry from a rugged, small-town sheriff.

McQuede didn't know how long he remained in the chair. He would probably have stayed there all night had not Psy let out another bark. McQuede rose and turned the rest of the now-cold hamburger over to him. Just as he did, the phone rang. McQuede glanced at the clock. Loris had probably been home for some time now. He scooped up the receiver, hopeful that the voice on the other end of the line would be hers.

"Sheriff, you've got to get here fast!"

McQuede could barely make out the distant, frightened words. "Who is this?" he demanded.

"Cory Coleman."

McQuede thought of the isolated ranch house, of Bartering Bill's old shed. "What's happened?"

"I was just attacked. Someone was hiding in the house. He sprang at me out of nowhere and—"

McQuede cut him off. "Are you injured? Do you need an ambulance?"

"No, but get here as fast as you can. I think whoever struck me is still lurking around!"

McQuede, siren screeching and lights flashing, sped toward Black Mountain, his mind racing as fast as the squad car. The attack on Bill Garr's nephew had taken him by surprise, a totally unexpected turn of events.

Whoever attacked Cory must still be after Bill Garr's treasure—the Pedro Mummy. That meant Bill Garr, before his appointment that morning, must have removed the mummy from the shed and hidden it in some safe spot. The murderer, believing he would find the mummy inside the glass case, had killed Garr for virtually nothing and was now in pursuit of what he had killed to possess.

Of course, this scenario was based on a questionable premise—Lex Wisken's testimony that the mummy did actually exist and that Bill Garr had just yesterday placed it in the display case in his store.

The flashing lights and sirens faded with the click of the car key as he pulled it from the ignition. McQuede stepped out into an eerie stillness. A dim light shone from the house, emphasizing the surrounding blackness, the weird shapes of the cliffs that rose directly behind the shed.

The scene looked surreal, bringing to mind shadowy little images from old Shoshone legends, of Wolf, the Creator; of Coyote, the Trickster; and of a mountainside filled with tiny, vindictive warriors armed with bows and arrows.

McQuede played the beam of his flashlight around the area. Tonight he fully understood the myths and legends that had sprung from the isolated canyons, and how a person could start imagining they heard mysterious voices or saw tiny creatures lurking behind rocks.

Cory met him at the door, gasping, "There's someone out here, I know it!"

"Probably not," McQuede replied calmly. "But the question is, did he get what he was after?"

"How would I know?" Cory took a few backward steps, his fingers exploring a spot just above his left ear. No blood showed on his head or on his hand as he dropped it back to his side.

Had he actually been attacked? McQuede saw no evidence of a bruise or swelling, but it was hard to tell though the ruffled hair. He stepped closer. "Let me have a look."

Cory shrank away. "I'm all right. At first the pain . . . was nearly unbearable, but now it's almost gone."

"I'll take you to the Durmont hospital."

Cory made no reply.

"A doctor should examine you," McQuede insisted.

"I'm not leaving here," Cory returned coldly.

McQuede stared at him for a while. Like it or not, he had to leave that decision up to him. "The front door isn't broken," he said. "How did he get in?"

"I already checked that. He broke a window in my uncle's room."

"Start from when you first pulled into the driveway, and tell me everything you can remember."

"I came home for my billfold, which I had left on the kitchen table. I saw no lights on in the house, nothing to warn me that someone was inside. As I crossed this room, I heard the sound of rushing footsteps from behind me. Before I could turn around . . ." Cory's hand went again to his head. "I was struck from behind."

"Can you describe the intruder? Did you get any impression of height, weight, the color of his clothing?"

"How could I? He sneaked up on me from behind and hit me hard."

"If he didn't find what he was looking for, he might try again."

The strange way Cory was acting, the vagueness of the details concerning the attack on him, his refusal to see a doctor, all served to arouse McQuede's suspicion. For the first time it occurred to him that Cory Coleman might not be telling him everything, that he knew exactly who had been out here tonight, and why. That meant Cory might have been in on the scheme to acquire the mummy in the first place. He might even have killed his uncle when he was caught in the

act of stealing it. If so, maybe Cory and the man he intended
to sell it to, likely the elusive professor, had in some way
fallen out.

McQuede made a circle of the room. His men had searched
through Garr's personal belongings, but his deputy would
never have permitted the house to be left in shambles. Drawers had been removed and dumped, cushions from the couch
and chair had been flung aside. Was that an indication of anger or merely a sign that the intruder had been in a frantic
hurry to complete his search? McQuede stopped beside the
closet near the front door. It gaped open, boxes overturned
and clothes dumped, hangers and all, in the center. "I'll post
a guard here tonight."

"You're wasting precious time. I tell you, I heard him outside, over near the shed!"

"Sirens have a way of making criminals vanish. But I'll
take a look."

McQuede left the house and stopped midway to the shed.
Murkiness obscured his vision, distorted the sagging outline of the old building. He thought of this morning, of Lex
Wisken and his prediction that darkness would spread over
the land Bill loved so much. As he stood motionless, the
sheriff sensed an evil so strong, he could feel its presence.

All of a sudden he detected a movement in the shadows of
trees beneath the rise of cliff. At first he thought the small
form was not real, just a ghostly manifestation of the old
Shoshone myth of the Little People.

But he knew better. This wasn't an apparition but likely a
flesh and blood killer, one who had struck down Bill Garr
and had a short time ago in the same manner attacked Bill's
nephew. "Coal County Sheriff!" McQuede shouted. "I'm
ordering you to stop!"

The figure set off running. He was heading straight for

the rocky cliff. McQuede fired a high warning shot. The bullet struck rock and ricocheted.

McQuede didn't know the lay of the land, whether or not a path wound up to the top, but he quickly pursued. Since he was unable to see the ground, his feet slid against loose stones, at times almost throwing him off balance.

At the bottom of the cliff, McQuede slowed his pace, fumbling for his flashlight and switching it on. He swept the light through the scrub pines off to the right. Convinced no one was there, he swung the beam to the other side, where someone could be lying in wait for him in one of those deep gullies.

At that moment, McQuede was alerted by a scattering of stones from directly above him. A barely visible outline, dark against the background of cliff, was scurrying upward with quick, panicky motions.

McQuede called to him. "Stop!" He fired his gun again, making sure the shot went far to the left. Even though the assailant must realize he was a sure target, that didn't stop him.

McQuede wasn't sure what to do now. Being on that path would leave him exposed, and he had no way of knowing whether or not the man was armed. But remaining here below would mean giving up what might be his one and only chance to apprehend Bill Garr's possible killer.

McQuede placed his gun in his holster and, using his hands to guide him, started to climb. He soon reached a wide trail, an incline that led almost straight up. Half-blinded, breathing hard, he continued to close the space between him and his quarry.

In spite of McQuede's best efforts, the man reached the top before he was able to catch up with him. The rest followed in rapid succession. First he saw the figure standing up, outlined against the sky; then he dropped to his knees.

Before McQuede fully realized what he was doing, he heard the thump of stone against stone and saw a big boulder plummeting toward him. He attempted to get out of the way, but he had no time. The rock hit his shoulder with a fierce impact that hurled him backward. McQuede rolled down the slope, pain jarring through him as his body struck earth and rock. Then pain and awareness vanished, leaving only blackness.

Chapter Four

McQuede lay sunken in darkness. Someone or something was standing over him. At any moment he expected to be bludgeoned to death, just as Bill Garr had been. He managed to open his eyes. As his vision cleared, relief flooded through him. The dreaded presence looming above him was merely a spindly pine.

The rock had bounced from the cliff and made a direct hit on his shoulder. He winced from intense agony as he struggled to his feet. He braced himself against the tree, working the fingers of his hand. Grateful, he realized he had sustained no permanent damage, no broken bones.

He wondered how long he had been unconscious. Time enough, he knew, for the person he had pursued to be long gone. Somewhere during the chase he had lost his cell phone. He'd go back to the squad car and call Sid Carlisle, as he should have done in the first place, and have his crew comb the area.

With painful effort, McQuede moved out into the clearing near the shed. The moment he emerged from the trees, he caught a glimpse of motion, a dark shadow disappearing around the building.

In spite of the shakiness of his limbs, he reacted quickly. Gun in hand, he rounded the shed. As he did, a shrill cry sounded, one hollow and distraught, like the howling of a wolf. A small form, seeming to appear from nowhere, lunged at him. As they struggled, McQuede lost hold of his gun.

His attacker—in the blackness the features took no shape—proved no match for him. The two rolled on the ground. Fingernails scratched his face, and blood trailed down his cheek. He freed his right hand to strike, but, aghast at the sight of his attacker's face, he did not. He broke free of the flailing arms and scrambled to his feet.

He fumbled for his flashlight and shone the beam directly on a frightened face. Her black hair curled in wild disarray above eyes that looked enormous, far too large for the thin face. McQuede had at first thought he was doing battle with a child, but now he recognized a woman, small and pixie-like, a somewhat larger version of the Little People in the legend. A woman! Definitely human.

He dragged her to her feet, where she struggled in his iron grip like a fish wiggling on a hook. "I'm arresting you for assaulting an officer of the law," he said gruffly.

She placed both hands over her face and began to cry. "This is all your fault," she wailed. "You shouldn't have been following me!"

He hadn't expected her reaction and was again astounded. "Just what are you doing here?"

"I . . . I wanted to get Pedro. Bill gave him to me, said if something happened to Bill, Pedro was mine to look after."

What else could take him by surprise? His attacker was not only a woman, but a crazy one.

Cory Coleman must have heard the shots, must have

known McQuede was in trouble, but he hadn't left the vicinity of the porch. When they approached, McQuede growled, "Here's your trespasser."

The woman's sobs grew louder.

"That's just Roma Fielding," Cory scoffed. "She lives in that old house just down the road." Even though Roma's large eyes were fastened on him, he tapped the side of his head meaningfully. "She couldn't have been the one who attacked me. Would you look at her? She wouldn't be able to hit me with such force."

"I'll have to disagree with you," McQuede said.

"But she wouldn't harm me, would you, Roma? She cares for . . . practically everything—birds with broken wings, baby animals that are orphaned."

"He's right." Roma had quit crying to smile. The smile made her look like some small, mischievous troll. "I wouldn't hurt anyone." She singsonged her statement again. "I wouldn't hurt anyone."

"The very idea is ridiculous," Cory agreed.

McQuede glanced from Garr's nephew to the woman dressed in faded T-shirt, jeans, and worn sneakers. Harmless, perhaps, unless provoked. Without question she had tried to harm him and could have attacked Cory with the same zeal. Even though she appeared small and timid, she did, in fact, have the capacity for violence.

"Why did you run from me?"

Roma Fielding, trembling like one of those scared rabbits she probably liked to rescue, brought her hands to her face again. McQuede took her thin arm, more gently now, and led her into the house. A pot of fresh coffee sat on the table. He poured Roma a cup and handed it to her. "Drink this."

She sank into the recliner, her breathing gradually returning to normal. When she looked up again, she was on the defensive. "You scared me!" she accused McQuede in a high-pitched voice. "That's why I ran."

"I've told you before, Roma," Cory said, "you shouldn't be wandering around after dark. It's not safe."

She set aside the mug and rocked back and forth. "Bill's dead. I needed to see you, Cory." She stopped, pointing a finger at McQuede as if all blame was his. "I cut across from the shed." Her voice rose higher. "I was on my way to the door. He came running out and started chasing me."

"Just calm down, Roma," Cory said. "Tell me, what did you want?"

"I want . . . Pedro. I'll be good to him. I'll look after him. That's what Bill wanted. He told me so. 'When I die, girl, he's yours.' That's what he said."

"Are you talking about that . . . mummy?" Cory exclaimed with disbelief.

"Strange," McQuede cut in, "that Pedro has turned up missing."

The news proved too much for her. Roma gave a cry of despair and began rocking again. "I let Bill down. I promised to care for Pedro. Poor little fellow. Where is he? What will he do now?"

McQuede and Cory exchanged glances. "Is there someone who can pick her up?" McQuede asked.

"I doubt it. Her mother died several months ago, and she lives alone."

McQuede addressed Roma. "Did you see anyone else out here tonight? Did you notice a car?"

"Anyone could come and go without being noticed," Cory answered for her. "There's endless places to hide a vehicle among all these clumps of trees."

Roma remained silent for a while, then burst out, "If Pedro's gone, I know who took him!"

"How would you know? Did you see someone take him?"

"*Lex* thinks Pedro is one of the Little People," Roma explained, as if this idea was much more absurd than her own beliefs. "Lex always said Pedro should be given a proper burial. That's what he did; he took him home."

"But Lex is the one who told me he was missing," McQuede countered.

"Of course he did," Roma said. "Lex did take him. That makes him missing, doesn't it?"

McQuede poured himself a cup of steaming coffee and took a bracing drink. Then he used Garr's office phone to call his deputy and explain what had taken place. "I might not be here when you arrive," he finished. "Just take Roma Fielding home and search the house again."

"Where will you be?" Sid asked.

"I'm going to talk to Lex Wisken," McQuede replied, replacing the receiver.

Cory had trailed him into the room. "While you were gone, I found something that might be important."

"What?"

"In Uncle Bill's room. I'll show you.

Cory lifted a book from the stack that had been shoved off a shelf and took out a folded paper. "I think this was overlooked by both your crew and whoever attacked me. This could supply the reason someone was in this house tonight. To find and destroy this."

The letter was dated last Wednesday, over a week ago.

Dear Mr. Garr,

*Word has reached me that you may be in posses-
sion of an artifact known as the Pedro Mummy. As
you may have heard, I have been searching for this
item, which is crucial to my research. I would like to*

set up an appointment with you at your convenience. If the mummy turns out to be authentic, I would be willing to offer fifteen thousand dollars just for the opportunity of examining it. Please keep this correspondence confidential, and do not show the mummy to anyone else before I have a chance to contact you again.

Sincerely,
Dr. Seth Talbot, PhD

Cory Coleman watched McQuede closely, a frown darkening his long, narrow face. "Do you know anyone named Seth Talbot?"

"Yes, I talked to Dr. Talbot after I left here today."

Talbot had lied to him. He did have an appointment with Bill Garr that morning. Now McQuede held in his hands the evidence he needed to tie the famous professor directly to the crime.

In the stillness, McQuede assessed what might have taken place. Perhaps Garr had refused to give Talbot access to the mummy, or else they had argued over the price. The professor in anger had hit him. Later Talbot realized he couldn't allow that incriminating letter to be found, a letter that would implicate him in the crime, so he had broken into Garr's house tonight to find and destroy it.

McQuede's namesake, the famous old lawman Jeffery McQuede, had often said, "When you're convinced you're right, it's time to step back and take another look." His gaze settled on Cory. A little too tidy, he thought. After all, his men had searched the house, and they wouldn't be careless enough to overlook any evidence as important as this letter

McQuede's gaze shifted from Talbot's note back to Cory, aware of his intense, almost wolflike expression, his eyes that for a moment seemed to flicker with some evil light. He had stakes in this game, all right. The missing mummy might not be the actual cause of the crime but a red herring intended to draw attention away from another, more common motive, that of cashing in on an early inheritance.

Lex Wisken's cabin was set against the mountain, perched on a tract of land that sloped steeply downward. McQuede's squad car, as if mimicking his weariness, seemed to slow of its own accord as the tires zigzagged around curves or locked into ruts.

Through straggly pines McQuede glimpsed Lex's brightly lit cabin, smoke billowing from the chimney. The land behind was a maze of corrals that Lex used to train horses. A huge barn was set off to the side.

Lex, alerted by the noise of the approaching vehicle, stepped out onto the porch, standing tall and tough-looking. "*Behne.*" Lex spoke the Shoshone greeting slowly, drawing out each syllable: *buh-nuh.*

The porch light magnified his pitted skin, and his dark eyes that narrowed as McQuede approached. Tonight McQuede could match Lex's rough appearance. His uniform was ripped and stained by the fall, and blood left by the scrapes of Roma's fingernails had dried on his face.

"Have you been here all afternoon?"

"Yes. I worked with the horses until dark."

McQuede stepped past Lex into a small room filled with the mingling smells of stew and wood smoke. A marred wooden table sat near the stove, and on the wall above it stretched a painted elk hide.

McQuede gazed at the blackened pot on the wood-burning stove, wondering if Lex had just made the stew or had left it simmering while he had taken a trip to Bartering Bill's ranch house.

"You look like you've been in a fight."

"I have." McQuede pulled one of the chairs away from the table and sank down, leaning tiredly forward. "With Roma Fielding, and she won."

"Battling Roma is like fighting unseen powers," Lex said, humor lighting his features. He wandered over to the elk-hide painting and tapped a hand on a crude outline of a man with raised war-club. "If someone tries to get in her way, Roma has the fury of a warrior."

"Or," McQuede replied, "of a madwoman."

Lex turned to him, the amusement gone from his face. "Roma listens to the spirits," he said. "That makes Roma less crazy than the people who poke fun at her." After a long silence he added, "Roma feeds the little animals. She wanders the mountains looking for the helpless ones, and she cares for them. A person with a cause fights. You must be standing between her and her goal."

"Would that goal be getting her hands on the Pedro Mummy?" McQuede asked. When Lex didn't answer, he told him about Cory's attack and the search of Bill Garr's house.

"Roma would not ambush anyone."

"She kept saying Bill Garr had verbally willed the mummy to her."

"Bill liked to tease her. He probably did say that, and she took his words seriously."

"Then what was the attacker expecting to find?"

"There are many answers. Money. His will. Valuables Bill probably kept in the house instead of the store."

"What if Pedro wasn't stolen by Bill's killer? What if he's still searching for the mummy? Do you think that could be possible?"

"When I left Bill, the mummy was in the display case. After Bill's death, it was gone. That's all I know."

"And you didn't take it?"

"If I'd found him, I might have carried him back to the Little People where he belongs, but I didn't."

As Lex spoke, he took a bowl from the cupboard, filled it with stew, and set it in front of McQuede.

McQuede said thank you gratefully in one of the Shoshone words he'd learned from Nate. "*Aishen.*"

Lex placed a heaping plate of fry bread and honey on the table and settled into the chair across from him.

"You're not going to join me?"

"I just finished my meal."

McQuede reached for the bread, warm and golden brown— his favorite from childhood, from hours spent with Aunt Mattie after school. He spread it with honey and savored the taste. The stew with its chunks of beef and variety of vegetables was strongly seasoned with onion and garlic. For a while McQuede forgot that he was there to question a suspect and not to seek solace and comfort.

Lex began reminiscing about the good years he had spent with Bill. His praise was sincere. Clearly Bill Garr had loomed a very large figure to him, a man to follow.

"I learned so much from Bill," Lex said. "He told me once, 'Find what you love to do, and put your whole heart into it.' I followed his advice and started raising horses, and that decision has made me a happy man."

Lex droned on. McQuede was paying little attention until Lex mentioned Bill Garr's nephew. "Cory's father was shiftless. His folks had nothing but what Bill supplied them. Cory loved Bill then. The boy was here all the time, underfoot. Bill took a lot of stock in him, like Cory was his son.

But he never got anything in return. Time after time, Cory let him down."

"Let him down? How?"

"I'll tell you a story that will help you understand," Lex said. "Over twenty years ago, Bill wanted me to move out to his land, and I did. That's when I began doing what I love most, raising and training horses. Bill wanted Cory to help me. For years he had dragged Cory along on his buying sprees, had make him mind the shop, but that didn't work for either of them. Cory never loved anything Bill loved— just his money and what Bill could do for him."

"You don't like him much, do you?"

"I did, once, a long time ago." Lex stopped short.

McQuede knew Lex intended to share some significant information with him. He waited, allowing the story to unfold in Lex's own way.

"The boy helped me then. The best time of my life, and of his too. We spent day after day with the horses. Back then the kid worked like a demon, but he hasn't worked a day since."

"When did he leave Wyoming?"

"After he graduated. Bill always gave Cory everything he wanted. He sent him to the university—why, I don't know. He never did anything with his education. He doesn't even have a steady job." Lex's voice became hostile, "Cory just sits around waiting for some 'get rich' scheme, so he can ride out the rest of his life without earning a living."

"I thought he was a consultant, working in geology."

"He works for Al Gaberille in Sioux City when he wants to, which isn't all that often. Cory wouldn't have survived a minute without the phone line to Bill."

"He did come back the minute his uncle got ill," McQuede reminded him.

"Cory probably told you that, but I'll tell you for sure, that wasn't the reason. Ten years ago the doctor said Bill needed a heart operation. Ten years ago he refused. Bill refused again, and who knows? He might have lived another ten years."

"Why did Cory rush back here, then?"

Lex leaned forward. "For money," he said. "Bill always told me everything. Cory had what Bill called some 'hare-brained scheme' and needed a lot of cash."

"What for?"

"To invest in some shaky gold mine venture in Nevada. Bill always knew a good deal, and this scam wasn't one. This time, Bill refused to back Cory."

"So he came back to talk his uncle into making the loan?"

"The minute he got here, they fought. Bill told me that Cory was never going to amount to anything and that he wasn't going to . . . what did he say? . . . keep throwing 'good money after bad.' "

"But Cory will inherit from him?"

"Yes."

McQuede slid his chair away from the table. He was assailed with images of Cory Coleman killing his uncle, bashing in his head like the Little People had done to the old and sick so long ago. But this was done not to alleviate Bill's suffering, not because he could no longer keep up with the tribe, but because Cory wanted an early cash-in of his inheritance.

Chapter Five

McQuede's shoulder ached. His night's sleep had consisted of an hour's doze before dawn, and he felt sullen and despondent. Loris had played a large part in darkening his mood. She hadn't even bothered to call him in an attempt to explain away her little outing with Arden Reed.

Sid Carlisle, neat and efficient, papers in hand, entered his office, took one look at him, and started out again.

"Hold on," McQuede said.

"This might not be the right time to discuss the Garr case," Sid replied.

"What do we have?"

"The coroner's report is just what we expected. Garr died from blunt force trauma. We searched the whole area and found no sign of the murder weapon."

"What about fingerprints?"

"No usable prints were found on the shed door. Too many people had come and gone. The fingerprints inside were legion, many of them Garr's. And as for the house, whoever had broken in made certain they left no evidence behind."

"Tire tracks?"

"Another dead end. Most of them match Garr's old truck."

McQuede grimaced as he leaned back in the chair. "I see. We're well on our way to solving the case."

Sid, overlooking McQuede's gloom, said, "I've been checking out that note you found beside Garr's phone. He had written a phone number and below that the word *appointment* and *10:30* is circled, but there's no way to tell if the two notations are related."

"What did you find out about the phone number?"

"Bud Lambert's home phone. He's the big investor who moved here last year from California and has been trying to buy Garr's property. Lambert claims he had."

"We'll have to check to see if he had set an appointment to talk to Lambert."

"I got a list of the other calls Garr made this month. One in particular caught my attention. About a week ago he placed a call to Terese Deveau."

McQuede pictured the woman he had met at the museum, one of the workers on Reed's project.

"Hope that gives you something to work on," Sid stated before he left.

Clearly Bill Garr had owned what someone wanted very badly, but it didn't necessarily have to be the mummy. McQuede lifted the paperweight on his desk, a gift from a friend of his, a Navajo policeman. The shifting of the multicolored sand always steadied him, always reminded him to keep seeing more than one pattern.

He'd have a talk with Bud Lambert and Terese Deveau, but right now Cory Coleman was of more interest to him. Recalling the name Lex had mentioned, McQuede drew the phone closer and asked information for the number of Cory's boss, Al Gaberille, from Sioux City.

"Al Gaberille speaking."

"Sheriff Jeff McQuede, Coal County, Wyoming. I need some information about Cory Coleman. I understand he's one of your employees."

"I wouldn't say that. My firm hires him on occasion as a consultant. May I ask what this concerns?"

"A background check, that's all."

Gaberille sounded relieved and immediately became less formal. "No need for you to worry. Cory's one of the good guys. His only fault is . . . a certain lack of ambition. He could work full-time for me, but he chooses only to show up when he runs low on cash."

"I've heard that he's been wanting to invest a large sum of money in some Nevada gold mine. Is that mine associated with your geology company?"

"I've owned and operated Gaberille's for twenty-five years." He gave a short laugh. "I've stayed in business by running crackpots like Ray Daniels off."

"A con artist, is he?"

"I wouldn't call him that. No, Daniels found a sprinkle or two of gold on his property and is dead set on launching a full-fledged mining operation. He kept talking to Cory, putting visions of glory into the boy's head, and finally he reeled him in. What people will believe when they want to! For a hundred thousand dollars Daniels offered to make the kid a partner. Co-owner of the side of an empty mountain, I'd say." Gaberille laughed again. "He tried to borrow money from me, but I flat turned him down. The only thing that'll save Cory is that he won't be able to get his hands on that much cash."

Cory may have found a way, McQuede thought, as he replaced the receiver. Wanting to check on the provisions of Garr's will, McQuede headed out to Bill Garr's ranch.

Cory reluctantly admitted him, demanding, "Do you know who broke in here yet?"

"I'm working on finding out." McQuede walked past him into the room. Cory had made an attempt to straighten up the house, but cushions were still askew on the couch, and once stacked boxes, old dishes and lamps spilling from them, remained upended around the hall closet.

Cory asked belligerently, "What do you want, then?"

"I decided to talk to you rather than Bill Garr's lawyer. You must know the provisions of your uncle's will."

Cory looked away, miffed. "I saw the original will early this morning." A muscle tightened in his jaw. "Lex sure chiseled me out of a good share of my inheritance. I had no idea he was going to get the entire north tract."

"Those two have been good friends since before you were even born," McQuede reminded him.

Cory seemed not to hear. "I don't know what Uncle Bill thought he owed Lex. He's supported the man all his life. Guess he wanted to keep on even after he died. Not much thought of my future, though. He didn't even care about what I might need."

"Not everything's about money," McQuede said.

Cory's reply, bound to be surly by the downward turn of his mouth, was cut short by a tap on the door. A heavyset man with the air of a balding Santa stepped robustly into the room. All smiles, he extended his hand to Cory, and then to McQuede. "I know you! The pride of Coal County, Sheriff McQuede. You've probably heard of me too, Bud Lambert. I invest in land."

Buyer and seller—they were wasting no time.

"Wanted to talk to you, Cory," Lambert boomed. "You probably don't know this, but Bartering Bill and I made a deal—why, the very day he died. I talked to him on the phone that morning, and he said I could buy the whole of his property, lock, stock, and barrel."

Vultures—the first to show up on the scene—and this one had an agenda. McQuede doubted that Garr had ever agreed to sell his property. It was easy to make misstatements about the dealings of a deceased man, and Lambert looked like the phony type who would do just that.

Lambert reached into his vest pocket, removed some papers, and held them up triumphantly. "Right after I talked to Bill, I made out this contract for the amount we agreed on. I just wanted you to know, Cory, I'm standing by my offer. I'll rewrite this identical contract, and it will be effective the minute you are legally able to sign."

Cory accepted the papers, frowned, and returned them. "I don't own the north tract. My uncle willed it to Lex Wisken."

"Bill never mentioned that to me. He told me he wanted to be rid of it all, every single acre." The jolly-Santa smile vanished from Lambert's flabby face. For a while he seemed at a loss; then his old manner returned, full force. "I'll tell you what I'll do, Cory." He stepped closer, the volume of his voice lowering to a confidential tone. "For you, I'll make an even better offer than I made him. I'll deduct fifty thousand from the amount of this contract"—he hit the papers against the open palm of his left hand—"and we'll just delete the north tract. That far exceeds what you'll get from anyone else."

Cory turned away. "I don't want to talk about this now. It's too soon."

But it hadn't been too soon, even before Garr was in his grave, for Cory to rush down to Garr's lawyer to find out just how much he was going to get.

"I haven't been able to come to terms yet with Uncle

Bill's death," Cory explained, his voice becoming thick and tearful.

"You think about it, son," Lambert returned, his manner preoccupied and devoid of sympathy. He fumbled in his breast pocket and placed one of his cards on the table. "We'll just keep in touch."

"We will too," McQuede said, and he followed Lambert outside.

They stood by Lambert's silver van with LAMBERT EN-TERPRISES emblazoned on the side. "You just talked to Garr on the phone?" McQuede said. "You didn't by any chance drop by to see him on the day of his death?"

"I intended to deliver the contract, but before I got the chance, I heard about what had happened. No telling what will become of our agreement now. That leaves me high and dry. I have big plans, and they all center around closing this deal without delay."

"You got in mind some land development project?"

"I always look ahead. Many of the rich folks I know are leaving the coast and moving to the mountains. They'll be relocating in rural areas just like this. I've made a lot of ar-rangements, have buyers lined up already." He stopped short and shook his head sadly. "I couldn't believe it when I heard some robber had killed him."

"There are lots of different kinds of robbers," McQuede said.

Lambert placed a hand on the car handle, but instead of opening the door, he faced McQuede again. "I live just a few miles west of here. I drive by this house several times a day." He paused, looking at McQuede speculatively. "This may be important, or it may not be. I'll tell you just the same. I passed by here about nine-thirty yesterday, and an old Ford convertible pulled around me and swung into Garr's driveway. With his reckless speed, he just missed sideswiping my van."

"Did you recognize the driver?"

"I did. It was that dealer they call Ruger."

Why did every crime committed in Coal County lead McQuede straight to his old enemy, Ruger?

McQuede stopped in Durmont at The Drifter bar, which Ruger's friend Sammy Ratone had recently purchased and had turned over to Ruger to manage. McQuede should have known he wouldn't find Ruger there. Ruger had no thoughts of going to work every day and usually poked the job off onto the barmaid, Sherry, or anyone else available so he could return to his first love, which was supposedly the buying and selling of cars and collectibles.

McQuede drove quickly, swinging left on the old dirt road that ended at the sprawling, ramshackle white farmhouse that had for years belonged to the Larsh family and was now owned solely by Ruger.

The property had gone steadily downhill since Ruger had taken over. The weedy yard was as crowded as Bill Garr's, crammed with sheds and outbuildings where Ruger stored his vast inventory. An old wooden barn housed the sports cars Ruger fixed up and sold as a hobby. Through the open doors he could see a beauty of a 1959 cherry-red Thunderbird convertible set up on blocks.

The smaller, locked buildings were filled with antiques, odds and ends, and probably stolen goods that McQuede suspected Ruger fenced to his friend Sammy Ratone in Vegas. McQuede wondered if the little mummy was hidden away in one of those locked sheds. He didn't have enough evidence to obtain a search warrant, and even if he did, by now the mummy would be long gone.

As he drew closer to the house, he saw that Ruger had a visitor. Sammy Ratone's sleek black Cadillac, looking out of place, was parked out front, next to the blue '93 Ford Mustang convertible Ruger usually drove around town.

"Come in, Sheriff!" a loud, boisterous voice called as McQuede stepped up onto the porch. "What did Ruger do this time?"

Sammy remained on the couch, dark glasses beside him, big stomach stretching the seams of his Mafia-like suit. A striped orange cat was perched on Sammy's lap.

The old tomcat that hung around Ruger's place wouldn't let anyone else near him but always slipped inside whenever Sammy appeared. The cat closed its eyes in bliss as Sammy ran a fat, ringed hand along its bristly fur. Selfish and greedy, they looked like two of a kind, as if they recognized kindred spirits.

Ruger emerged from the kitchen, hands raised in mock surrender. "Don't shoot. I'm innocent."

"I haven't told you why I'm here yet," McQuede said in a no-nonsense voice. He didn't like the games these two played with him, making something humorous out of what was immensely serious.

"I'm all ears."

"Then maybe you can tell me why your blue Mustang was seen entering Bill Garr's driveway the morning he was killed."

Ruger shrugged. "I stopped by Bill's around nine or ten, trying to sell him the same stuff I sold to Nate. For some reason or other, Bill wasn't in his usual bartering mood. He told me he just wasn't interested."

"Why didn't you tell me this before?" McQuede demanded, regarding him with narrowed gaze.

Ruger's blue-gray eyes met his with insolence. "You never asked."

"That was before I knew you had been out that way. What happened to your ironclad alibi?"

"I guess I made that up," he said, smiling, "because of the way you're always freely accusing me. But I will tell you for sure, when I left, the old man was alive and kicking. You can ask Cory Coleman. He saw me talking to his uncle from the window and waved to me as I left."

Cory had mentioned that someone had pulled into the driveway, but he had claimed that he hadn't looked out. One of them wasn't telling the truth. If Cory was lying, that might indicate that Ruger might have been there to see him, that he and Ruger were working together—possibly on procuring the mummy or on some other illicit deal. If Ruger's statement was true, that didn't rule out the possibility that he had returned later and attacked Garr.

"I'm told the little Pedro Mummy is a one-of-a-kind item, something certain people might kill to get their hands on," McQuede said. "Maybe Pedro's hidden in one of those locked sheds out there."

"You bring a search warrant, McQuede?"

"Sure you didn't take it to fence to your pal here, in Vegas?" McQuede gestured to Sammy. "That why you're here, Ratone? To pick it up? Maybe you have it in the trunk of your car right now."

"Ha! A *mummy*?" Sammy Ratone looked both amused and indignant. "McQuede, you blame me for everything. Ha! What am I going to do with a mummy?"

"I've heard there are people who would pay top dollar for it."

"Not my clients. A diamond—now, that's another story. Maybe a rare painting. Everything I acquire is legal and aboveboard, of course."

He remembered Ruger saying that if he had the mummy,

he would turn it over to Sammy. McQuede knew that wealthy collectors sometimes got a taste for the macabre, like the ones who bought serial killers' art, such as the clown paintings John Wayne Gacy had created on death row. Despite his protests, the sheriff had no doubt Ratone, with his high-roller connections, knew just such unsavory people, and where to sell such an item on the black market.

"Maybe I can ask around," Ruger volunteered. "I get to all the flea markets and shows. Someone's bound to know something." His speculative gaze turned on McQuede. "You'll make it worth my while, won't you? If I could find something out?"

"You know I don't operate that way. But I'd think it would be in your own best interest to be off my list of suspects."

Ruger considered this. "I don't know who stole the mummy, but I might be able to help you track down where it went. There's this old trader up in Cody, Jonas Finney, who used to buy and sell to Garr. At one time the two of them were rivals, always trying to outdo each other. I'm making a trip up that way soon, so while I'm there, I'll see if the mummy has turned up in that direction."

With much effort, Sammy hoisted his weighty form from the couch. The cat, annoyed by the sudden motion, jumped from his lap and leaped to the nearby chair. Sammy dangled a set of car keys in front of McQuede. "Sure you don't want to search my car, McQuede?"

"Not necessary," McQuede replied, knowing that if Ratone would allow him to check the trunk, he would find nothing more than a jack and a spare tire. But that didn't mean he was innocent.

"Then I'll be on my way to my office."

McQuede knew his local "office" was The Drifter bar, where he imagined he conducted all kinds of shady deals.

Ratone made a show of brushing cat hair from his baggy suit trousers. "Darn cat. I'm a human hair ball." But his voice was gruff with affection.

Ruger reached down for the cat and scratched him carelessly behind the ears. With an offended look, the animal scrambled out of reach and darted behind the worn brown sofa. "I'm the one who feeds him, but he won't have anything to do with me," Ruger complained. "He only likes Sammy. Now, tell me, is that fair?"

"Better get a dog," McQuede advised. "At least they're loyal."

"I don't like dogs," Ruger said.

Loyalty, McQuede imagined, wasn't high on the list of Ruger's sterling qualities.

Chapter Six

At the Coal County Museum, the stuffed black bear, snarling and poised for battle still looked formidable. McQuede stopped short, gripped by the illusion that this rugged creature was standing between him and Loris Conner.

The front door to the museum opened, and Arden Reed entered, movie-star handsome in an expensive jacket that matched the touches of gray at the temples of his black hair. Looking neither right nor left, with his expression cold and stony, he hurried by McQuede.

McQuede managed to speak pleasantly. "Good morning, Dr. Reed."

Reed didn't answer, didn't so much as glance toward him. A strange reversal of attitudes—McQuede should be the angry one; after all, Reed was the one trying to steal Loris away from him. McQuede watched as he cut through the large commons area and disappeared into an adjoining room.

To McQuede's disconcertment, he found the door to Loris' office closed and locked. He wandered around trying to locate someone friendly enough to ask about her.

Terese Deveau sat behind the same computer screen in the large common room, studying what appeared to be the same set of petroglyph photos, as if she hadn't moved since McQuede had come into the museum looking for Loris late yesterday. Only her clothing had changed. Today she wore a casual denim jacket, and her tied-back hair revealed tiny turquoise earrings that added a feminine touch to her otherwise no-nonsense appearance.

She looked up at McQuede, amber eyes lighting in recognition.

"Always busy," McQuede observed.

She smiled. The smile sparked an attractiveness that he would otherwise have overlooked.

"I'm one of those people married to work."

"A replay of my own life," he answered, sinking into one of the folding chairs across from her. "Have you seen Loris?"

"She's out at the site."

"Actually, I need to talk to you too. You know I'm investigating the murder of Bill Garr. His phone logs show that he placed a call to your cell phone number on a Friday, a week before his death."

Terese did not hesitate. "He did contact me. About Dr. Talbot. He wanted to know how to get in touch with him."

"Where did Garr get your number?"

"From the museum newsletter, I suppose. Since I'm working freelance on this project, I listed my personal number."

"I understand that at one time you were assistant professor to Dr. Talbot. Have you kept in touch with him since you left the university?"

"No. In fact, finding out we were going to be scheduled to work together on this project came as quite a surprise to both of us."

Terese's quickly averted gaze suggested that the surprise

wasn't a pleasant one, and from what he'd seen of Talbot, McQuede could well believe it.

"What did you tell Garr?"

"I told him Dr. Talbot would soon be in Durmont. I also supplied him with the New York phone number where he could be reached."

"Did he tell you why he wanted to contact Talbot?"

"I didn't know what he wanted or whether or not he followed up on it. Of course, in retrospect, I realize he must have wanted to talk to Dr. Talbot about the ad Talbot had placed concerning the Pedro Mummy."

Word had gotten around that the missing mummy could have been the motive for the crime. No doubt, by this time, Arden Reed and others on the museum staff had discussed it at length.

It was beginning to look as if Talbot had arranged to meet with Garr, had kept the ten thirty appointment Garr had written on his notepad. McQuede had sensed an aggressive impatience in Seth Talbot that could easily explode into rage or violence if someone stood in the way of what he wanted. It would follow that the two men had argued, maybe over price, or more likely because Garr had changed his mind about showing or selling the mummy.

McQuede cast Terese a sidelong glance. "Would you mind giving me your opinion of Talbot?"

This time Terese did hesitate. "A while back, as an undergraduate, I thought he could walk on water." Once again the amber eyes avoided his. "That changed. Later, we worked together, dated. Luckily, before the wedding bells sounded, I was able to see him as he really is." She didn't speak for a while, then added, "As arrogant as he is, he didn't take the rejection well."

"No one does," McQuede replied.

At that very moment the closed office door across the room from them flew open. Reed stomped out, Talbot's loud voice booming after him, "You're not coming in here accusing me! You misplace a few papers, and who do you blame? That's why you hired me in the first place, to be a scapegoat. What makes me responsible for everything you bungle?"

Reed stopped in his tracks, then whirled back to face off with Talbot. "One more warning, Talbot. If you have any complaints about my management of this project, you take them up with me."

"If you'd do your job right in the first place, I wouldn't have to go over your head."

"You turn everything into some horrible publicity stunt," Reed said under his breath. "But not this. I'm running this show."

Talbot fairly yelled, "There wouldn't be any project if it wasn't for me!"

McQuede rose. For a moment he thought the polite, soft-spoken Arden Reed was going to start a physical battle.

Reed worked hard for control. "You will come up with some answers soon if you want to stay on this team."

Talbot glared after Reed as he walked back through the commons area and into the museum proper. Talbot then returned to his office, slamming the door shut behind him.

Terese Deveau and McQuede exchanged glances. "Trouble on the project?" McQuede said. "Think I'll try to find out what it's all about."

"I can fill you in on that," Terese said in a hushed voice. "Seth Talbot just keeps causing trouble. A few days ago he went behind Dr. Reed's back and filed a complaint with his superiors in D.C. concerning the way he's been managing the project."

"What complaints did he cite? Do you know?"

"Talbot accused him of everything from refusing to delegate authority to the mismanagement of funds."

"Are any of the accusations true?"

"No, none of them. Talbot's played this trick before. At the university, he became chairman by undermining the head of the department. He's discrediting Dr. Reed in the same way."

"Will Talbot's complaints be investigated?"

"If they are, Talbot's sure to come out on top. He can be . . . quite convincing." She finished with caution, "In fact, I had second thoughts about joining the project when I found out I'd be working with him. So far I've survived by managing to stay out of his way. He only crushes those who oppose him."

McQuede rose, smiling. "In that case, I think I'll go in and try my hand at opposing him."

McQuede tapped on Talbot's door. "Sheriff McQuede. I need to talk to you."

"Another time," Talbot said irritably.

McQuede opened the door and stepped inside.

Talbot made a display of ignoring McQuede as he shuffled through a desk drawer. When he looked up, his eyes, made more prominent by the heavy brows, settled on McQuede, ice cold. With his ruffled dark blond hair, his bristly beard, and safari jacket, he looked like a hunter just returning from an expedition.

"I'm very busy. If you have something to say, say it."

McQuede took his time. He drew the letter signed by Talbot from his jacket pocket and handed it to him. "Bill Garr's house was broken into last night. We found this hidden inside his study. It looks as if someone was attempting to get back what could be incriminating evidence."

Talbot skimmed the message, unable to conceal the look

of surprise that flitted across his face. "I remember writing that letter," he snapped, "but I never mailed it."

"It's strange, then, how it ended up in Garr's possession."

"That's impossible!" As if he had been struck by some revelation, he stared at McQuede. "Unless . . . I do know how it got there! And, if I'm not wrong, you know too."

McQuede made no reply.

"I wrote this letter before I knew how soon I'd be joining this project. When I found out I needed to be in Durmont soon and I could contact him in person, I never mailed it. I must have tossed it into my briefcase with my other papers, papers that someone has been riffling through at will."

"So how did it get into Garr's study?"

Talbot's challenging gaze held McQuede's. "I think you know, McQuede. You're helping Reed set me up!"

McQuede did not reply.

"Don't play innocent. You're working right with Reed! Don't think for a minute I don't know it. It's an outright attempt to frame me!"

"Are you accusing Reed?"

"Yes! With your help. I assume you searched the place after Bill Garr was murdered. Strange, this letter should just turn up now. Maybe whoever broke into Garr's house last night didn't plan to steal anything but to plant this letter."

"So you believe Reed is in the process of framing you? Why do you think he'd do that?"

"For money, lots of it. He's as greedy as they come, mostly for fame."

Talbot seemed to be labeling Reed with his own major sin.

"No doubt about it, Reed intends to be the one to cash in, to write the book I've planned—about the Pedro Mummy."

On their last visit, Talbot had accused Barry Dawson of wanting to do the same thing.

"Reed now has his hands on the mummy. He'll figure out some way to make it reappear, after I'm booked for murder! After that, his career, which has been dead-ended for years, will skyrocket. He'll be a man of international fame. But why am I explaining this to you? You're helping him! You're on Arden Reed's payroll!"

The mean-spirited accusation was hardly worth denying. McQuede didn't bother.

Talbot regarded him sharply. "What do you get paid, McQuede? I know a small- town sheriff like you would leap at the chance to earn some big money."

McQuede gave a dry laugh. "Money does come in handy, doesn't it? Look what it's bought you." McQuede said the words sarcastically, but Talbot read envy into them.

"So, there, you admit it!" Talbot got to his feet, big and menacing, like the black bear in the display room.

"I should never have advertised my willingness to pay for information on that mummy. This mistake of mine has escalated out of sight! Look what's happened! Reed has killed Garr, stolen the mummy, and is now framing me for murder!"

Back in the common area, McQuede stopped to ask Terese Deveau, "Do you have any idea where I might find Arden Reed?"

"He had plans to meet Loris at the petroglyph site," Terese answered.

"Can you give me some directions? It's been a while since I've been out there."

"It's pretty remote, in the heart of Black Canyon. You start toward Paxton, then about fifteen miles down the blacktop you turn off on Bad Creek Road. If you keep going, it will soon become little more than a dirt trail. In time you'll see a sign that reads Lost Cave. If you don't have a four-wheel drive, you'll have to walk from there up the mountain trail to the summit."

As he left the building, McQuede spotted Arden Reed in a silver Toyota Land Cruiser, sorting through his briefcase. He tapped on the window.

"What's going on between you and Talbot?" McQuede asked.

Reed, an angry air still hovering over him, replied, "It's a private matter."

"Not when I'm investigating the murder of one of our local citizens. I've just talked to Talbot. He believes you've stolen Garr's mummy."

"What nonsense. I'm not a thief. If I wanted it, I would have outbid him."

"He thinks you invited him into this project to set him up and take over his book about the Pedro Mummy."

"He does, does he? And that makes it true?"

"I'm willing to listen to your version."

Reed thought a moment, then, as if making a difficult decision, said, "I've been long obsessed with the theory that the Little People actually existed. When I came here from Washington, D.C., I brought with me years and years of my own personal research. Some of my important papers have come up missing. Where do you think they went? Talbot's been pilfering them to use in his fool book!"

"You don't have any proof of that, do you?"

"They would be of immense importance to him, but I won't be able to prove him a thief. Neither will I be able to prove that a lifetime of research belongs to me."

"Just don't do anything about it," McQuede advised. "Let me work behind the scenes and see what unfolds." McQuede started away. "I'll want to see you later today. Right now I'm going out to the cave site to talk to Loris."

"When you see Loris," Reed called after him, "tell her I won't be able to make it out to the site today."

McQuede's sense of unease increased even before he reached the Durmont city limits. The total isolation added to his apprehension, the deeper he drove into the canyon. The highest peak in the Black Mountains range soon loomed directly above him. The blacktop came to an abrupt stop. He continued on a deeply eroded road that was barely passable. When he spotted Loris' vehicle, he parked beside it near the sign LOST CAVE and began walking up the steep trail.

Despite the buzz about Talbot's book, the place had never become a popular tourist spot—the climb was too rugged, the cave too remote for any but an occasional archaeologist or an extreme petroglyph enthusiast. Probably weeks went by, even in the summer, with few or no visitors.

Loris, lost in concentration, was kneeling by one of the stone carvings at the entrance to the site. She looked so care-free, the way her honey blond hair blew loose in the wind. He didn't call to her, just drew closer.

When she looked around, she gasped. "Jeff. You startled me."

McQuede looked closely for a smile, for the light that often came into her eyes when she saw him. "Guess you were expecting Reed. He told me to tell you he won't be able to get out here today."

Instead of voicing her disappointment, she said, "I'm a little jumpy, I guess. I keep getting the feeling I'm being watched. I did spot someone on that cliff over there."

McQuede gazed toward the jutting outcropping of rock in the distance.

"I think maybe it was Barry Dawson. He was wearing those khaki clothes Barry wears when he hikes. But I called to him, and he just disappeared."

"How long ago was that?"

"A while ago. I don't know." She brushed at the hair the wind had blown in disarray. "A person loses track of time up here."

"I don't like your being out here alone. In fact, I think you ought to quit this project. You're putting yourself in danger."

"I think your job is more dangerous than mine. Maybe you're the one who ought to quit."

McQuede, ignoring her retort, told her, "Reed got into a fight with Talbot this morning."

"No one gets along with Dr. Talbot," Loris replied.

The tone of her voice indicated that she, too, might have had a run-in with him. "Arden, on the other hand, is easy to work for, very fair-minded. If there's trouble between them, you can be sure Talbot is to blame."

"Don't get too fond of Reed until I check out some of Talbot's accusations," McQuede warned.

"Speaking of Arden," Loris said, drawing herself up, "he's very important to my career. He's handed me a once-in-a-lifetime opportunity, and I didn't like how rude you were to him at the restaurant."

"So, I'm imperfect. I thought you knew that."

A small smile flitted across her lips, sparking light in her hazel eyes. "That you are," she proclaimed with what he thought was a hint of affection.

"What do you say you forget your studies for a bit and show me around the site?"

Loris looked pleased that he had taken an interest in her work. "This way. The grand tour awaits."

McQuede trailed after her.

"Like him or not, Dr. Talbot made a very important discovery when he located this cave."

"I've seen caves with Native American drawings before. What makes this one special?"

"Because so many years of history are represented by the rock art found here."

Loris pointed out, chipped into the wall of an overhanging cliff, faint images of what looked like men, elk and bison, winged creatures that resembled birds.

"Here you can find two types of art. Petroglyphs were made by pecking and carving designs into stone," Loris explained, indicating the image of a warrior etched into the rock. She pointed to another image, a circular shape in faded black and red pigment. "Pictographs are designs painted directly on the stone."

To McQuede, most of the drawings seemed an indefinable blend of animal and human. "That one looks a bit like a turtle," he commented uncertainly.

Loris laughed. "Interpreting rock art is a little like describing cloud formations. Not everyone sees the same shape. But in this instance, I think you're right. Let's go on up to the cave."

With Loris beside him, McQuede barely felt the ache in his shoulder as they began to ascend a steep wall, broken up by worn foot and handholds.

McQuede didn't know just how far they had climbed until he looked down. Far below, he could see the tops of junipers, the small stream that meandered through the canyon bed. He watched a hawk vanish into the blue sky, leaving a peaceful silence in its wake.

As they reached the dark entrance to Lost Cave, Loris clicked on a flashlight. She stepped inside, stopping to trace a shallow carving lightly with her fingers. "These scratch-style carvings near the entrance were made by the Shoshone within the last two thousand years," Loris said. "They scratched their designs over the existing petroglyphs to drive out the magic of the earlier ones."

"I wish it were that easy to alter the past or the future."

Loris pointed out a drawing and said with sudden enthusiasm, "I do recognize this likeness. It's *Pa waip*, a water ghost. "See the long hair fashioned in braids and the tear that streaks her cheek? She was believed to wail and cry to lure men into the water to drown."

"Not a very nice spirit," McQuede commented. "Sounds like a siren in Greek mythology."

"Yet the water ghosts can be also be helpful, especially in times of war. Warriors with water ghost powers could cure battle wounds."

McQuede was impressed by her knowledge. As he trailed after her deeper into the cave, the light from the entrance diminished. "Why do you think they left these drawings on stone?" he asked.

"All people have a desire to record their history. Obviously some of the drawings were made to mark important events. Others are believed to have been created to communicate a spiritual message. To many tribes these caves are sacred— *poha kahni*—places of power for visions."

They had reached the darkest point, the end of the cave. "This is what I want you to see." She played the beam from the powerful flashlight across the rock, allowing the light to bounce along a series of smaller, fainter carvings in stone. "These are the ancient ones. Notice the absence of horses. The oldest of these rock drawings are believed to be made by the direct ancestors of the Shoshone, possibly dating back to over two thousand years ago." She gave a little laugh. "Of course, there are those who believe these early rock drawings were made by the Little People."

The carvings here were much different from the ones near the front of the cave. McQuede studied the small, compact shapes of tiny, skeleton-like humans carrying spears and bows.

"What do you know about the Little People?" McQuede asked, suddenly very interested in hearing her academic, unbiased account.

"Tales of Little People were part of Native American legend long before the Europeans arrived," Loris told him. "They are part of the oral tradition of many tribes, including the Arapaho, Sioux, Cheyenne, Crow, and Shoshone. In some tribes, the Little People were regarded as hostile. In others, they were believed to be spirits or beings possessing magical powers, like leprechauns or fairies."

"Nate told me the Shoshone called this race of tiny people the Nimerigar," McQuede said. "To the Shoshone, they were mostly hostile."

"Yes, their legends tell of Shoshones being attacked by their tiny bows and poisoned arrows." She lowered the light, leaving the walls bathed in sinister darkness.

"There have also been stories of hunters being led astray with their calls and becoming lost, but this was not always on purpose. The Little People can be a vocal bunch. At night it is believed you can hear them wailing or beating sticks against the trees." After a pause she added, "There are some among the elders who claim their spirits live on in hidden places. Some still think invisible arrows are the cause of accidents and all kinds of misfortune."

"But I also heard that catching a Little Person might be good luck," McQuede said to lighten the somber mood. "Maybe we should give it a try."

He became aware of her smile, although her features were obscured. "Even among the Shoshone, the tales vary. Maybe the Little People are much like us, a mixture of good and bad. All I know is, you have to respect them or suffer the consequences." Her voice had changed, taking on the animation of a child telling campfire tales. "Some believe that looking at the drawings angers the Little People. They say you can hear the carvings talk at night."

An eerie feeling swept over McQuede as he gazed at the images in stone. The tiny shapes seemed to shift before his eyes, the stick-figure men brandishing their bows menacingly. McQuede wasn't a superstitious man. Still, he had a sudden desire to leave this place before the rocks started whispering their displeasure and he felt the sting of a thousand tiny, invisible arrows.

Chapter Seven

McQuede kept thinking of the man dressed in khaki clothing who had been watching Loris. He had no intention of leaving her out here alone. "Why don't you gather your belongings, and I'll follow you back to town."

To his surprise, Loris agreed. She lifted a backpack from beneath one of the rock carvings and shuffled through it. "That long climb made me thirsty." She took out a canteen, shook it, then upended it, but not a drop of water came out.

"We'll stop at the café for one of Mom's cherry Cokes."

She made no reply, as if her thoughts had drifted to some faraway place.

McQuede, afraid that he knew where, said, "I wonder why Reed didn't show up here today."

She glanced away. "Probably he had car trouble. Normally, I take the project's Land Cruiser, but it wasn't working right, so Arden told me to take his Jeep. He must have run into problems with the repairs."

Now she was driving Reed's car. Trying to contain a flare

of jealousy, McQuede reminded her, "You don't know him very well."

"Arden and I met over a year ago at a conference in Denver. After that, he kept in contact with me. I have to admit, I found that flattering, for he is so highly esteemed in his field."

McQuede had tried to convince himself that her association with Reed was just work-related, but that was getting harder to do. Loris spoke too highly of him. And just now— he had noticed it before—she avoided meeting his gaze when she mentioned his name.

Still not looking at him but gazing out across the canyon, she said, "Arden wants a romantic relationship, but last night I told him about us."

The vast sky, clear and blue, the way the rugged land was sprinkled with bright autumn colors, no longer looked inviting to him but cold and remote.

When he made no reply, she said lightly, "I'll lead the way." She began carefully maneuvering around jutting stones toward the little trail below them. Once the ground leveled off some, she increased her pace, moving far ahead of him. The rocky path dead-ended at the dirt road where they had parked their vehicles, and Loris reached it before he did.

There, she drew to a startled stop. "Jeff, what's happened to Arden's Jeep?"

McQuede, feet sliding, hurried down the slope to join her. The windshield had been shattered, probably by one of the large rocks lying nearby. All four tires on the Jeep had been slashed. McQuede's squad car had suffered the same fate. In addition, someone had ripped out the dispatch radio and had flung it to the ground near the back bumper.

"Who would do this?" she asked in a voice startled and disbelieving.

McQuede instinctively reached for his cell phone, knowing all the while he would get no signal. They were probably twenty or thirty miles from the nearest cell phone tower or any sign of civilization. McQuede went to the back of his vehicle and lifted the radio.

Loris drew closer. "Is there any chance of fixing it?"

"Whoever did this made sure there wouldn't be."

"Jeff, we're stranded here! What are we going to do?"

He tossed the radio into the squad car and turned to Loris. Aware of her fear, he tried to lighten her mood. "Not all is lost. We can eat berries and . . . can you make a fire by rubbing sticks together?"

She ignored his attempt at humor. "The man I spotted early this morning must have done this, but why?" She looked around apprehensively. "He's probably still out here."

McQuede scanned the area, the thick trees and looming rocks that encircled them, and any attempt at levity vanished. If this was an ambush, they were going to be helpless targets.

"You say Reed usually drives the Jeep? Maybe he's the one this was planned for and not you."

His statement served only to add to her worry. "You told me Seth Talbot and Arden got into a fight this morning. That man has a terrible temper. He could have done this to get even with Arden."

"That would be sort of a childish act," McQuede remarked, "for a professor."

"There'd be more to it than that. What if it were Talbot I saw out here this morning? What if he's working on his own, trying to beat us to some answers? If so, he's likely to do everything he can to sabotage the project."

"What sort of information would he be after?"

"Both he and Arden are trying to link the ancient drawings I just showed you with the theory of the Little People."

"Talbot had access to the cave long before the rest of you. He's the one who discovered it. Why would he be doing that now?"

"He could have found a new connection from Arden's research," Loris replied. "You don't know that man. He certainly doesn't want to be a team player. He's all for himself. He's disrupted everything since the minute he arrived."

McQuede remained silent for a while. "What about Reed? I told him I was coming out here. Any possibility he got caught up in some jealous rage?"

Loris' voice held an edge of anger. "You can't mean that. Arden's the most mature man I've ever met. There's nothing petty or mean or envious about him."

McQuede's heart sank at her words, at the way she was defending him so wholeheartedly. He turned away.

"Shall we set out walking?"

"We're too far from help."

"We could see how far we would get driving on the rims."

"I already know the answer to that," McQuede replied. "We'd be better off staying here."

"But no one will show up until tomorrow."

"Don't worry. Someone will drift out this way eventually." With great effort McQuede smiled at her. "In the meantime, it might be fun spending a little time together."

He wished that were so, that they were two people in love, that this strange situation hadn't arisen. His gaze warily swept across the isolated mountainside. This may not have been a petty act of revenge but a plot to isolate them here.

Uneasiness settled around them, hovering like the mist that had formed over the creek. Not sure of what to do, they remained near the disabled vehicles.

Because of the high elevation, the brisk autumn air would

soon grow unbearably cold. Despite her heavy sweatshirt, Loris had already begun to shiver.

"We're going to be stuck out here all night," McQuede said. "Are there any provisions in the Jeep?"

"Let's see what we can find." Loris opened the back of the Jeep, calling, "There's a sleeping bag."

McQuede took his flashlight from the squad car, and in the glove compartment he found a book of matches. Holding them up to Loris triumphantly, he said, "We can start a fire."

"No food, though."

"At least we can use your canteen to boil some water."

McQuede headed toward the creek, with Loris trailing after him. Near the bank, he made a circle of rocks. He gathered wood and soon had a roaring campfire. Loris filled the canteen with creek water and watched as he positioned it over the flames.

"There's no one I'd rather camp out with than you," he said, chuckling.

She didn't seem so keen on the idea. "It'll be so dark once the sun goes down."

"Don't worry, we have fire. It will keep the animals away, everything away . . . except for the Little People."

"Jeff, you're just trying to unnerve me."

She looked so girlishly slender in jeans and sweatshirt, her thick hair hanging wind-blown around her shoulders. He wanted to take her into his arms, to rid her of all her fears, but he instead went back to arranging wood on the fire.

He allowed the water to boil until he was certain it would be safe to drink, then placed it aside to cool. After a while he rose and handed it to Loris, saying with another smile, "Poor man's coffee."

She took a sip. "Thanks, Jeff. I was getting really thirsty."

"I'm getting hungry. Too bad we don't have any marshmallows to roast."

"You're always hungry," she said. As if some thought had just occurred to her, she began searching through her backpack. "Look what I found." As if by magic, she produced two granola bars. "Dinner is served."

"At least we won't die of thirst or starvation," McQuede said.

Loris spread the sleeping bag on the ground, and they sat together, backs resting against the rocks, feet warming by the fire. The heat felt almost cozy. McQuede slipped an arm around Loris and was relieved when she did not pull away.

They ate and passed the canteen back and forth. All the while McQuede, without making a point of it, kept alert watch around them.

"So you think this is related to Bill Garr's death?" Loris asked suddenly.

"Likely it is. That mummy of his did turn up missing."

"But he wouldn't have to have been killed by one of the people on the project. One of them might have taken the mummy, but I don't think any of them would commit murder to get it."

"From what's at stake, they might. It looks as if there's a race going to get a hold of new evidence for that Little People theory. Have you uncovered anything new at this site?"

"The caves are hardly treasure troves. Nothing in them but the drawings."

"Then drawings it must be."

"There's nothing they can remove from here," she insisted.

"But the drawings can be photographed and analyzed. They can be used in a book or paper to support a theory."

"This information has been accessible to anyone for over a year," Loris protested.

"Then we're dealing with some new discovery."

"None I know about."

They soon fell silent. Coldness and darkness had fallen in earnest.

Loris, looking uncomfortable, slumped against the rock. Time passed slowly. Eventually, Loris, weary by the long day, leaned her head against his shoulder and closed her eyes.

McQuede, too, felt the grueling effects of the past few days. His entire arm ached, his injury affected by the damp air. He would have liked to close his eyes too, but he didn't dare let down his guard. If Loris was right, and Talbot had come out here to seek petty revenge, he was probably long gone by now. But he couldn't take the chance that someone remained, lurking around, watching them, waiting for the dead of night to strike.

Whoever had sabotaged their vehicles might be the same culprit behind the vicious murder of Bill Garr. The fact that they had also damaged the radio led him to believe that they planned on returning when he and Loris were most vulnerable. But why?

Grateful he had his gun with him, McQuede remained wide awake, keeping watchful vigil. He could hear the night sounds, the rustle of small animals in the brush, the continuous gurgling of the creek.

McQuede began to identify with his great-uncle, the famous lawman he so revered. He imagined old Jeffery McQuede holed up in some isolated canyon waiting to be attacked by some gang of outlaws. And now, here he was, over a century later, gun balanced on his knee, waiting for a face-off with some unknown enemy.

Time crept by without his fears materializing. He sat in the darkness, watching the crackling fire. In the quiet, the rush of wind through cracks in the rocks began to sound like faint murmurings. He knew now how the legend that the stone carvings could speak had gotten started, for the sound reminded him of hushed, almost angry whispers.

In the darkness it was easy to imagine they were being watched. He could almost hear the sound of sticks beating against the trees, of tiny voices wailing. Images of Little People brandishing arrows flitted through his brain. Then of Bill Garr, his skull smashed by some cruel weapon.

Feeling uneasy, McQuede glanced up. As he did, he caught a glimpse of a dark form silhouetted against the cliff by the pale wash of moonlight. The figure looked both small and yet large and looming.

McQuede, gently moving Loris aside, leaped to his feet.

The shadowy form, not that far away, seemed frozen as it stared down at them.

Loris stirred. "What is it? What's happened, Jeff?"

"There's someone up there."

As quickly as he had appeared, the watcher vanished behind a huge boulder.

McQuede grabbed his flashlight, looping it around his wrist, then drew his gun. "You go back into those trees and hide," he said to Loris. "I'm going up there."

She scampered to her feet. "No! I'm coming with you. You'll need my help. I know the area better than you do."

His own fears doubled. He now had to be concerned not only about facing this potential danger himself, but about protecting her. Yet he had no time to persuade her to stay behind, even if that were possible. "Stay near me," McQuede said.

He focused the beam of light downward, trying to avoid

tangles of foliage. Ahead of them a loose rock fell, hitting the ground intermittently. It brought back memories of Roma and of the impact of stone slamming against his shoulder.

Loris had no trouble keeping up. "Let's try to get close enough to make an identification."

After a strenuous climb they reached a ridge, which kept narrowing. They proceeded cautiously toward a huge, jutting rock that blocked their way. Beneath it, the wall dropped straight down into the canyon.

"Beyond this boulder the path forks off," Loris said breathlessly. "One trail continues up the cliff, the other drops down into the meadow."

McQuede halted for a moment, playing his light upward. Whoever they were pursuing might have *wanted* to be seen. He felt a strong warning; they could be falling into some trap. Once they got to the other side, they could find someone waiting, gun aimed and ready. "Taking this path is too risky. I'm going alone from here. Can you make it back to the cars?"

McQuede didn't wait for her answer. He holstered his gun and took a deep breath. He found an eroded area in the limestone to place his foot. Finding a handhold, he hoisted himself up. Careful not to look down, he used his left hand to raise the flashlight that dangled from his wrist. Finding another deep indentation in the stone, he braced his foot and reached above him to grasp a crack in the rock. The movement caused a sprinkling of stones to tumble down the side of the cliff.

"Be careful!" Lois gasped.

Cautiously, with tedious slowness, he inched his way forward and with relief planted his foot on solid ground.

He turned to announce his success to Loris and to his horror found her following his lead.

"No, Loris! Go back!"

Loris, lighter and more agile than he, moved faster, more confidently. He could do nothing to make her turn back now. He forced himself to remain motionless. If he went out after her, that would only cancel whatever chance she had. He watched in agony, expecting that at any moment she would make a misstep and plummet to her death.

Loris was midway now. After she took one more step, McQuede gripped the slab of rock and extended his hand to her. Once she was safely in his arms, he didn't want to let her go.

"Look, Jeff. Below us!"

To McQuede's surprise, the person they were following hadn't headed toward the high cliff but had abruptly changed course, doubling back toward their camp. McQuede gazed down the plateau where the land gently sloped into a meadow and caught a flash of movement just below.

They hurried downward until they could hear the rippling of the shallow stream that cut through the canyon. After a while McQuede halted, alerted by a rustle of branches just ahead of them. He directed the light through a cove of trees. It illuminated a glow of khaki clothing.

"This is Sheriff McQuede!" he yelled. "I'm ordering you to stop!"

The only answer was the resounding of his own voice.

"Over there!" Loris cried.

With Loris beside him, they began racing in pursuit. The fleeing form had reached the creek. They could hear the splashing of water. Before they arrived at the bank, a motor revved. Through the mist they made out the faint image of a car speeding away.

"Oh, no!" Loris moaned.

McQuede felt the same overwhelming disappointment. They had given it their all, and it hadn't worked. Without speaking, they followed the creek, intercepting their make-shift camp. The fire was flickering out, but a light shone through the trees from the place where they had parked their cars.

"There's no way we can follow now," Loris gasped.

Switching off the flashlight, McQuede led the way through the darkness toward the road. The outline was not of the car they'd seen but of a pickup truck. Someone was emerging from behind the wheel.

"Someone's headed toward the Jeep," McQuede said.

"Don't make a move!" McQuede ordered, stepping out of the trees. He approached, gun drawn, ready to fire.

Terese Deveau turned to face him, her amber eyes glowing wide and frightened like those of a startled cat.

Loris called from behind him, "Terese, thank goodness it's you! Look what's happened to our vehicles."

McQuede quickly replaced his weapon, feeling as if Terese was the posse that had arrived just in time to save them.

Terese stopped to gape at the destruction done to Reed's Jeep.

"They slashed the tires to Jeff's car, too, and destroyed the radio."

"Such rage," she said with disbelief. "It's scary."

"Oh, Terese, I'm so glad you're here."

"When you weren't back by five, I got worried," Terese replied. "I called your home but got no answer. I waited at the museum for a few more hours, and when you still didn't return to lock up, I was afraid you'd had car trouble. So I've been out looking for you."

"I'm so glad you did." Loris filled her in on their dangerous chase through the cliffs. McQuede watched her, proud of her courage. No wonder he loved her.

Terese accompanied them back to their makeshift camp. McQuede quenched the fire, and Loris rolled the sleeping bag and lifted her backpack. "I can't wait to get home," she said wearily.

The three of them climbed into the truck. The dashboard light illuminated Terese's thin, heart-shaped face. The crinkles around her eyes had become more apparent, and deep frown lines altered her appearance.

Terese drove skillfully, allowing the wheels to follow the deeply eroded tracks. They soon reached the blacktop. McQuede, with relief, leaned back against the seat.

Terese's voice broke the silence. "Who do you think vandalized your vehicles?"

"I don't know. Yet," McQuede replied. "We just missed being able to identify him."

"Could you tell anything about him, his height or weight?"

"He was wearing khaki-colored clothes. That's all I was able to see. It was impossible to tell who he was, but I know he has some connection with our project."

"I think you're right," Terese said, "judging from all the fighting that's been going on. None of this is Arden's fault," she added ruefully, "the troublemaker is definitely Seth Talbot."

"I had a little talk with Reed out in the parking area at the museum, but Talbot was still in his office. Did you see him leave?" McQuede asked.

"He left shortly after you did," Terese replied. "I tried to talk to him as he cut through the conference room, but he walked right by me without saying a word."

"Did you see him after that?"

"No, he didn't return," she said, "and I was glad for that. You should have seen the look on his face. I've never in my life seen a man so angry!"

Chapter Eight

McQuede's Aunt Mattie called midmorning insisting that he meet her for lunch at the Mom and Pop Café. Busy as he was, McQuede had no thought of refusing. During the short drive from Durmont to Black Mountain Pass he prepared for the appointment by recalling his mother's constant advice: "Jeff, try not to irritate your Aunt Mattie." That had been a full-time job during his growing-up years when he had worked for the Malones at their newspaper office.

A large sign set in the window displayed his bid for re-election. McQuede hadn't had time to campaign, and the date was drawing near. He stopped to regard it: VOTE JEFF MCQUEDE, COAL COUNTY SHERIFF. A tough, unsmiling face, resembling those on a wanted poster, looked back at him.

Mattie and his cousin, Darcie McQuede, sat at one of the checkered-clothed tables in the center of the room—the center, of course, for that's where Mattie always chose to be. Her tall, angular form leaned forward anxiously, intense black eyes watching McQuede as he strode toward them. She made Darcie, with her long brown hair and wide, innocent eyes, seem very young and fragile.

Darcie smiled at McQuede shyly, glad to have an ally in whatever battle or mission Mattie was launching.

"I've ordered the special for you," Mattie said, her appraisal becoming critical, as if he were hours late instead of precisely on time.

With her soft, silver hair and well-sculpted features, she should appear gentle instead of intimidating

"How's the murder investigation coming along?" Darcie asked politely.

"Not as well as I'd like."

"I hope that changes," Mattie cut in. "I went to school with Bill Garr. We were always good friends."

"They tell me Cory is here in town," Darcie said.

Again Mattie meddled. "Now, there's someone to be looking at. Bill told me that boy was always difficult. I myself would never trust him."

In one of her rare moments of voicing disagreement with Aunt Mattie, Darcie said almost firmly, "Cory's different than he appears. He just isn't one of those people who fit in easily. In high school he was always a loner."

"That's usually the description of someone who doesn't abide by the law."

"Not necessarily," McQuede drawled. "It's my experience that criminals come in many types. They're scientists and councilmen; they're writers and historians, just like Aunt Mattie."

"Don't be comparing me to Cory Coleman. Bill said just the last time we talked that, despite all of his education, Cory couldn't even hold down a job."

McQuede thought of his reelection and what Mattie would think of him if he got voted out of office. "A job doesn't define a man," he replied. He managed to meet her unwavering gaze.

"Mind my word, Jeff. Cory is someone to be watched."

McQuede glanced away from her, feeling a jolt as his gaze fell upon Cory Coleman. He was seated at a back table talking intently to a man who hadn't bothered to remove his black Stetson.

"I don't suppose he plans on staying here," Darcie was saying a little sadly. "Cory will never meet Durmont's strict standards."

"Speaking of Cory," McQuede said in an undertone, "he's right over there."

Mattie turned. At the same time Cory's voice drifted toward them, low and somewhat threatening.

"I'm beginning to see why Uncle Bill didn't like dealing with you."

McQuede suddenly recognized the man Cory was addressing—Ruger. Once again McQuede felt electrified, as if he were witnessing thieves falling out. Were the two of them involved in some kind of conspiracy? Images swarmed through McQuede's head—of Cory hiring Ruger to steal the mummy. Or worse.

Cory, without a glance in either direction, headed to the cashier, paid the bill, and walked out of the café.

The waitress came with the fried chicken.

A short time later, as if allowing Cory wide berth, Ruger pushed back his chair. As he sauntered by their table, he paused to tip his hat, all unpleasantness forgotten. "Mornin', ladies, Sheriff. Or should I say afternoon?"

"I do believe it's afternoon, dear boy," Mattie replied, beaming at him.

Ruger always turned on his charm for Mattie, who, to McQuede's amazement, seemed totally taken in by him.

McQuede was surprised that women found Ruger so attractive, but it must be so, judging from the way his cousin Darcie's wide-eyed gaze met Ruger's, then, flustered, dropped away.

Today Ruger wore hand-stitched cowboy boots, tight jeans, and a western shirt that highlighted the unruly locks that tumbled over his forehead. Both women reacted to the angelic face framed with golden hair but seemed oblivious to the coldness in his blue-gray eyes. They didn't know Ruger as McQuede did. They never had to confiscate the .357 Blackhawk he often carried or interrogate him over crimes that the sheriff was certain Ruger had a hand in but couldn't quite prove.

Ruger flashed Darcie a winning smile. "Who's this pretty little filly?"

"I thought everyone knew my niece, Darcie," Mattie answered proudly. "She's the head librarian for the Coal County Library."

"Now, isn't that a shame? I don't get to the library much," Ruger drawled.

McQuede almost scoffed aloud at the understatement. He doubted Ruger had read a book in his entire life.

"A man's got to earn a living." His eyes roved over Darcie with bold approval. "But maybe I'll make it a point to visit our local library more often."

"That Frank Larsh is such a nice young man," Mattie said later, after Darcie had gone back to work.

Mattie was about the only one who called Ruger by his given name. Years ago she had been friends with his mother, Nona, who had belonged to her garden club. McQuede had to admit, Ruger's parents were well-respected. Too bad Ruger hadn't maintained their high standards.

"Handsome, too. The spitting image of his rodeo-star

father." Before McQuede could wonder where this was all leading, Mattie, who loved to play matchmaker, said with a sparkle in her eyes, "I have half a mind to set him up with Darcie."

McQuede's voice held an edge of outrage. "Do you want to ruin the poor girl's life?"

"You saw for yourself the way those two young people were exchanging glances."

"Ruger's not that young."

"Neither is Darcie. She's almost thirty. She needs a good man in her life."

"A good man, maybe. Ruger doesn't fit that bill."

"I wish you wouldn't call him that."

"The name suits him. Just take my word for it, he's dangerous. He corrupts everything he touches."

"Oh, now, Jeff."

How could Aunt Mattie, so intelligent, so practical, be deceived by someone like Ruger, the town's most notorious rake? The mere thought made him angry. Knowing the pitfalls of carrying on with this discussion, he lifted the bill from the table. Mattie, who always insisted she pay her share, meticulously counted out the exact amount.

McQuede did get in the last word. "Just leave Darcie alone. She's got a good life ahead of her, and that man would ruin it."

McQuede was surprised to find Barry Dawson in the commons area of the museum occupying Terese Deveau's chair in front of the computer. He looked different, today, having changed his immaculate gray suit for a khaki safari outfit. "I see you're working on a new image," McQuede said.

Dawson laughed. "A man gets tired of looking like a stuffy professor."

The crisp khaki clothing couldn't help reminding Mc-Quede of Loris' words, linking the man she had seen on the cliff with Dawson. "I suppose since you're so interested in the project, you've been out visiting Lost Cave."

"No, I haven't been out to the actual site since Talbot discovered it a couple of years ago. But I plan to make a trip soon."

"What brings you here today?"

"Terese," he replied proudly. "She's asked my opinion on choosing some petroglyph examples for the Denver exhibit." Dawson showed him a close-up photograph of the double body of a human with one set of feet. "Very unusual example of a petroglyph in the Dinwoody tradition."

Dawson lifted another blown-up photo of what looked like a small figure atop the head of a larger figure. "Also rare."

"These very old?" McQuede asked.

"Hard to say. Dinwoody refers to a certain style of petro-glyphs found around the lake of the same name in Wind River. Some are only a few hundred years old, others over two or three thousand. Terese could tell you more. She's the expert on radio-carbon dating."

"What, exactly, does she do up in Casper?"

"Her regular work involves facial reconstruction and identifying skeletal remains. But her first love is Native American studies. She worked with Dr. Talbot, you know, at the time the local petroglyph cave was first discovered. Terese," he said, "is such an intelligent woman. We share so many interests."

The way Dawson spoke her name caused McQuede to look at him closely. A certain sparkle appeared in his gray eyes that gave him away.

"Don't tell me you've been struck by Cupid's arrow."

Dawson laughed. "Better than one of those invisible

arrows Nate talks about." His handsome face suddenly sobered. "To tell you the truth, McQuede, I could use some advice."

"I'm your man."

"Ever since Margaret passed on, I've been alone. Not that I mind, but I think I've found a person I would like to spend some time with. Terese is so interested in my Native American collection, in everything I love. I've been thinking . . ." His voice faded away. "I've been out of the dating scene for so long, I just don't know exactly what . . ."

"Just invite her out as if it were no big deal," McQuede said importantly.

"That's easy for you to say."

"And bring her a gift. Not flowers. Terese doesn't look the type. Stop by Nate's and pick up one of those Shoshone beaded necklaces. If I'm any judge of women . . ."—McQuede made it sound as if he were—". . . she'll take that bait."

"I don't know. I may lack the nerve."

"Most of all, make your invitation sound exciting." McQuede slanted him a skeptical glance. Dawson wasn't going to be able to do that. Most of the time he was as dull as a wooden knife.

Dawson adjusted his rimless glasses and leaned back in the chair. "How do I do that?"

McQuede changed his voice to a shrill falsetto. " 'Tonight I'm going to the Shadow Mountain Inn to dine and dance. Would you like to join me?' "

At that moment Terese walked in. She hesitated, a look of surprise on her face. Dawson sank deeper into the chair.

Quickly their attention turned toward the back office. The door had been flung open, and Arden Reed was fairly shouting, "You're through here, Talbot. You're fired, as of now!"

"You can't fire me! What a fool that would make you. I'm

the one the crowds will be flocking in to see. I'm the one who discovered the cave, or have you forgotten?"

Reed's voice was coated with ice. "You're not funding this project. You're not directing it, either. From this moment on, I am denying you further access to the site and to all of our records."

"You'll regret it if you do!" Talbot yelled. "I have power in your little circle. I can ruin you! Just wait and see. When I get back to New York, where will your precious funding be then?"

All of them watched agape as Seth Talbot stormed by them and out of the museum.

Terese turned to Reed. "He's right, you know," she said. "Maybe I should talk to him."

"I don't care what happens!" Reed shot back. "I won't work with that man again!"

McQuede, thinking he would catch Talbot before he left the parking lot, started after him. Reed called him back. "Wait a minute, Sheriff. I need to speak to you . . . in private."

McQuede followed him into the office the two men had just left. Reed, visibly shaken, seated himself behind the desk. He brushed a distraught hand through his hair, then looked up at McQuede somberly. When he finally spoke, his words were calm and steady. "I want to report a crime. I told you yesterday how Seth Talbot had stolen years of my personal research. That, I could do nothing about; it would be his word against mine. But now Talbot has pilfered valuable files belonging to the Smithsonian, papers entrusted to me. I will not be blamed for a theft he committed."

McQuede regarded him. He attempted to put aside his personal grudge against Reed and treat his complaint as he would any other. Yet in the back of his mind, he wondered if there were any papers or if this was just a petty grievance against Talbot that Reed had cooked up to reap revenge for some old score. "What, exactly, is in those files?"

"Links that may show a tie-in between the newly discovered cave drawings and the Pedro Mummy. It's the basis for my own research. For years I've interviewed the local Shoshones, all of whom are long dead now. I recorded their comments about the Little People, which that scoundrel plans to claim as his." Reed's dark eyes changed as he spoke, growing harsh and vindictive. "If I have to stop him myself, he's not getting away with it!"

"If you're willing to sign a complaint against him, I'll get a search warrant."

"We don't have time for any delays," Reed said. "If I know Talbot, this very minute he'll be packing. Once he's on a plane for New York, I'll never get those items back."

"When I confiscate the work, you will need to identify it."

"In addition to a paper here and there, he has lifted several bound files. They will be marked as belonging to the Smithsonian. There's a registered record that they have been released under my name."

"I'll see what I can do."

McQuede found Seth Talbot in the parking lot of the Grand View Hotel. He had arrived not a second too early; Talbot was leaving Durmont, likely for good.

"Dr. Talbot, Arden Reed has reason to believe you may have some papers in your possession that are property of the Smithsonian." He showed him the search warrant. "I'd like to ask you to step out of the car."

McQuede had expected boisterous objections, but Talbot obeyed without a word. This morning he wore a heavy forest-green sweater and tan trousers, the casual attire standing in contrast to his Rolex watch and the large signet ring that in a dashing swirl of gold displayed the initials s.t.

His compliance suggested one of two things: either Talbot was innocent of the crime, or he had already mailed the papers off to his New York office or in some way disposed of them. McQuede doubted that he would find incriminating evidence in the car, any more than he would have in Sammy Ratone's.

"Would you open the back?"

Talbot pressed a button, and the trunk of the rental car, a big Lincoln, swung open. Inside were neatly arranged file boxes and suitcases.

"I know what you're doing, but you're not going to find anything," Talbot said, his words rapid and cross.

McQuede lifted out an expensive-looking leather bag. Behind it, looking different from the rest of the load, sat a large, oddly shaped cardboard box bound with mailing tape.

"This is absurd." Talbot stopped short, sputtering, "Humiliating! I know nothing about Reed's missing papers. He'll be hearing from my lawyers, and so will you."

"I'm only doing my job."

"See if you have one long."

McQuede placed the oblong carton on the ground.

"What is that?" Talbot demanded. "It certainly isn't mine! I don't pack in cardboard boxes."

Expecting to find Reed's valuable research, McQuede stripped off the tape. He stared down at a small object wrapped in a blanket as carefully as if it were a newborn baby. McQuede unwrapped the covering of cloth and froze— face-to-face with the Pedro Mummy.

Chapter Nine

Seth Talbot stared down at the mummy with what appeared to be genuine shock. "A setup! That's what this is!" He drew in his breath and said indignantly, "Arden Reed is responsible. He's set me up!"

A possibility—Reed had been furious, and this could be a way of getting even with a hated enemy. On the other hand, Talbot, packed and on his way out of town, had no reason to believe that he would be detained. He could expect to get away safely, the mummy tucked away in his car.

Irritably Talbot checked his expensive Rolex. "I have plans to be in Casper by six. If you'll remove that . . . thing . . . from my trunk, I'll be on my way."

"I'm afraid you're not going anywhere, Dr. Talbot. Except down to the station with me."

"You're not going to arrest *me!*"

"It's no secret you were offering fifteen thousand for information on the Pedro Mummy," McQuede said. "Unless you can explain how this stolen property got into your vehicle, you're going to be booked for grand larceny."

"I'm no fool! Only an idiot would place incriminating evidence in his own car!"

"Not much risk, since you were leaving town. If Arden Reed hadn't reported those papers missing, you'd be gone, and no one would be the wiser."

Talbot stepped forward aggressively. Once again he reminded McQuede of Hemingway, the great hunter, firmly fixing his sights on some unsuspecting prey. "Did you find any of his precious papers? No, I didn't think so. What does that tell you?" His hard gaze locked challengingly on McQuede. "Reed's trying to frame me for a crime he committed!"

"It wasn't Reed who had planned to meet with Bill Garr." To drive home the seriousness of the situation, McQuede added, "An innocent man who was bludgeoned to death in his store."

"You can't believe I had anything to do with Garr's death." Talbot's eyes had changed, had become narrow and calculating. "I can supply you with plenty of cash if you will make all this go away."

McQuede responded to the statement with acid silence.

Even in the face of open refusal, Talbot continued promoting his offer as if he were conducting business as usual. "You know the reward I was offering for the mummy. It's all yours. All you have to do is make this unpleasantness . . . disappear."

"For your sake I'm going to forget I ever heard that," McQuede replied coldly.

"You don't mind playing the game with Arden Reed," Talbot said huffily, "why not me?"

"I have no idea what you're talking about."

Talbot, as McQuede had seen him do before, launched a full-blown attack. "I was right about you from the first. You've been paid to protect Reed. You have been working for him from the very beginning."

"Don't be reversing our roles. I'm not the one facing charges."

"You soon will be!" Talbot stepped even closer in a gesture of obtaining total control. "I won't go down alone. If I have to play dirty, I will. I'll bring the lot of you down with me."

Not responding to Talbot's threats, McQuede began reading him his rights.

"Where is Talbot's little stowaway passenger?" McQuede asked Sid Carlisle. While McQuede had dealt with Talbot, who had persisted in his assertion that he knew nothing about how the mummy had gotten into the trunk of his car and had insisted on not saying another word until he spoke to his lawyer, his deputy had taken charge of the tiny mummy.

"I sent it over to the coroner's office," Sid replied.

"It's a little late for his services, isn't it?" McQuede said with a short laugh.

"The coroner thought so too. He told me archaeological matters were not in his job description."

"What happens now?"

"When I delivered the mummy a while ago, he told me he'd asked the local professor, Barry Dawson, to recommend an expert. He said one has been working here on temporary assignment. That woman from Casper. What's her name? Terese Deveau? She's down at the lab now."

"Guess Terese is the logical choice for the job," McQuede said. "I'll just go over there and see what she can tell us."

McQuede liked to avoid the coroner's office as much as

possible. The sight and the smell of the place reminded him of all the accident and murder victims he hadn't been able to save.

No corpses were being examined that afternoon, for which he was grateful. The little mummy in his permanent cross-legged position sat upright on a steel table like some ominous gargoyle. His bronze-colored skin and compressed features reminded McQuede of pictures he had seen of the bog men in Ireland.

Terese stopped her work and looked up at him. A beaded necklace, a medallion of dark blue with yellow stars, contrasted with the white lab smock she wore. An air of excitement sounded in her greeting. "Am I glad to see you."

"What have you found out?"

"Over here. I'll show you."

McQuede was no doctor, no scientist. With an inward shudder, he hoped she didn't expect him to examine the mummy. The thought of even touching it made McQuede recoil.

To his relief, she bypassed the mummy and led him to a small worktable. A large computer screen displayed two sets of X-rays placed side by side. McQuede recognized the almost transparent skeleton of the little mummy, the slightly curved spine, the flattened head, the tiny ribs.

"The original X-rays of the Pedro Mummy have been archived for years. I had images sent to me to compare to the new X-rays, which I just scanned into the computer. Look at both of them together. What you see is going to amaze you, amaze the entire world!"

As she spoke, her fingers toyed with the beaded necklace. He had seen it before, in the display counter at Nate's Trading Post. Dawson had lost no time following his advice. He had selected a star motif, a symbol of the idealistic approach to the work they both shared. In fact, Dawson would give anything to be standing beside her at this moment. He should be here instead of McQuede, a small-town sheriff who saw Pedro as a victim instead of as a source of knowledge.

"Take a close look. Tell me what you see."

"The two X-rays look identical."

"That's because they are!" As if overwhelmed, Terese sank into the chair, silently gazing at the images the way children do at Christmas trees. Finally she said with awe, "We have found the long-missing Pedro Mummy! This is the same mummy Dr. Shapiro examined in the fifties."

"I thought he might be a fake," McQuede remarked.

She seemed not to hear him, her mind lost to other concerns. "See in both copies the complete set of ribs and teeth?"

"And that means?"

She tapped the screen for emphasis. "Every detail, from the unusual position of the body right down to the damage to the skull is the same. This proves he's the original Pedro Mummy."

"The one Bill Garr had hidden away in his shed for all these years."

"From its first discovery scientists have been trying to determine whether the Pedro Mummy was a full-grown man or the remains of a deformed infant. The original X-rays were re-examined by scientists in the seventies, but by then the mummy had disappeared. Without it the experts could come to no real conclusion. This is definitely not an infant suffering from anencephaly. The evidence is all there—the full set of teeth, the closed fontanels."

Seeing that she had lost him, Terese explained, "Soft spots in the skull that grow together as a person reaches adulthood." She glanced up at McQuede, expecting him to share her exhilaration. "Do you know what this means?" Without waiting for an answer, she said, "These are the remains of a man about sixty-five years old, definitely not a child. There's no doubt in my mind," Terese Deveau finished with a breathless rush of words, "that not only are we looking at the original Pedro Mummy but that he was a full-grown man when he died."

Despite his innate skepticism, McQuede felt a sense of amazement. "So this . . . little mummy . . . could validate the theory Talbot is so eager to prove in his new book."

"It appears he was on the right track all along." The light that gleamed in her amber eyes reminded him of Barry Dawson's when he was on the trail of some new theory. "This could turn out to be the most important find in decades," Terese exclaimed. "It supports the idea that an unknown race of tiny, prehistoric men once lived in this area."

"The Little People." It took McQuede a moment to take in the significance of it. "So what happens next?"

"I'm making arrangements to transfer Pedro temporarily to the lab in Casper tomorrow."

Talbot had to have known this mummy was authentic. The knowledge that it was not a fake made the possibility that Talbot had murdered and stolen to obtain it far more likely.

"What will happen to the little mummy once it reaches Casper?" McQuede asked.

"Many experts will want to examine him. More examinations will be performed, advanced DNA testing conducted. But not at the Casper lab. Most likely, an important find like this will be turned over to the Smithsonian."

And right into the hands of Arden Reed. McQuede thought of Reed, whom he didn't trust any more than he trusted Seth Talbot. "We'll keep Pedro here until he can be safely transported." He added, "For security reasons, let's keep all information concerning the Pedro Mummy between you and me. Don't discuss the fact that he's been found or share any of your findings with anyone, not even with Dr. Reed."

Even though Talbot was in custody, McQuede wasn't willing to drop his investigation. He decided to stop by Ganion's Sinclair to see if the problem with the project's Land Cruiser was the reason Reed hadn't met Loris at the site.

Gus Ganion, drying his hands on a rag, stepped away from the Land Cruiser when McQuede entered the garage.

"Haven't made the repairs yet?"

"That would be a feat," the old man said. "He just brought it in this morning."

McQuede had found out what he'd wanted to know; now he'd locate Reed and ask him where he had gone after fighting with Talbot at the museum.

Before he reached his vehicle, his cell phone rang. Without identifying himself and with no preparatory remarks, Lex Wisken announced, "We've got a problem, one we must deal with right away."

"What's the . . . ?"

A click sounded on the other end of the line, resounding and final.

Reluctantly, for he had wanted to question Reed, McQuede headed toward Bill Garr's property. Still unable to settle on some reason for Lex's call, he quickly swung the car to the left, winding upward toward the Shoshone's cabin. A silver van lettered LAMBERT ENTERPRISES was angled close to the porch.

The source of the problem became apparent—an argument, perhaps over a land deal. Not knowing what to expect,

McQuede bolted from the squad car and hurried to the door, which swung open just as he approached.

Standing close behind Lex, the land investor, Bud Lambert, boomed, "So we meet again, Sheriff."

McQuede passed by them deep into a room warmed by a blazing fire in the woodstove. He turned back slowly. *Vulture,* he thought, as he faced Lambert. The label seemed extreme, considering the benevolent beam on Lambert's happy face. He glanced from one man to the other. "What's the trouble?"

"No trouble between Lex and me. We're in total agreement." Lambert turned toward the big Shoshone. "I have another appointment, so I can't stay. I'm pleased that you're considering my offer, Lex. You'll never get a better one."

Lex stood in the doorway, watching the van until he could see it no longer. "He doesn't know refusal from acceptance," he said.

"You have to give him some credit; he doesn't waste a minute putting in his bid."

"I guess not. They haven't even probated the will yet." Lex paused solemnly. "Lambert says he's going to build high-priced houses all around me. I told him, even if he did, I intend to stay right here, me and my horses."

"I've seen his sort before," McQuede replied. "He'll first try to stop your dealing in horses here. He'll go to the commissioners and do all he can get this stretch of land rezoned."

Lex did not respond to McQuede's warning, and instead said, "But Lambert's not the problem. I called you out here because of Roma."

"Roma?" McQuede chuckled. "I'm not sure I want to tangle with her again. What's she done?"

Lex firmly closed the door and walked by McQuede to

the window. For a long time he stared out at the thick trees that dropped down into a steep ravine. "She's out there now."

"Why?"

"I think you know the answer to that. She thinks I have the Pedro Mummy, and she wants it."

"She's . . ." McQuede was going to say *harmless* but changed his mind. "Can't you just ignore her?"

"I first saw her last evening. I went out to talk to her, but she ran away. Then she came back. She's been out there all night."

"What is she doing?"

"Waiting, watching, probably for a chance to search my house."

"Like she did Cory's?"

"I believe someone else besides Roma attacked Cory," Lex said, "even though she was out there too. That's why I'm worried about her. She might know who did."

Silence fell around them.

"In any event," Lex said, "she shouldn't be spending the night outside. The mountains get very cold this time of year. She doesn't take care of herself."

"I don't suppose she ever has, but there's little I can do about that."

"Tell her to stay off my property."

McQuede reached the door, then paused to remind him, "There's not much I can do. If you're serious, you need to bring trespassing charges against her."

"I wouldn't do that," Lex said. "Roma's my friend. I understand her."

"Then fill me in."

Lex's voice became low and mystic, "She loves the earth, the sky, the forest. She loves the wind that gusts through the branches, the earth-smell of rain, the scent of pines. Most of all she loves the little creatures and looks for those who can't take care of themselves. Now she has become one of them. She needs your help."

"I'll see what I can do," McQuede said.

He walked around the cabin, surveying the lay of the land. To the west lay a vast stretch of flat pasture, dotted with corrals and encircled by a fence that enclosed the finest horses McQuede had ever seen. Not far behind the house loomed the dark shelves of reddish rock. Roma would be somewhere east, close enough to set up a post where she could view the cabin. He concluded that his search for her would be useless, for by now she would have been alerted by the squad car and fled.

A cascade of small rocks slid under his weight as he descended the slope. The bright sun had taken coldness from the air, but he still felt a damp chill. Hard to imagine that Roma had maintained vigilant watch throughout the night.

McQuede descended into a deep gorge, crossed it, and began climbing upward again. From this vantage point he saw the layout of Lex's property below, the curls of smoke lifting into the air.

He walked along the top ridge, then, in surprise, drew to a stop. Roma was seated on a log, staring through scrubby pines toward Lex's cabin. "Roma."

At first he thought she was going to jump to her feet and scamper away, but she remained, huddled in place, not looking at him. She wore a tattered jacket that must have done little to protect her against autumn's early frost.

"I'm going to take you home," he said gently.

"I am home."

"No, you are on Lex Wisken's land." He didn't know how to advance his opposition, for he had no past experience to draw upon. The people he had confronted, even those who had committed heinous crimes, acted from some kind of logic that he could at least comprehend. He said sternly, "Trespassing is a crime. A person has a right to privacy. You have no choice but to leave here and not return."

Roma compliantly walked ahead of him down the mountainside toward the squad car. Once inside, she shrank against the door, as far away from him as possible. "There's another reason I don't want you out there. Bill Garr was murdered. It's not safe for you to be wandering alone in this area."

His counsel was not making any connection. She did not speak a word to him as they pulled up to her old, two-story house.

"Roma, do you have any idea who killed Bill Garr, or who broke in and attacked Cory Coleman?"

If she did, she wasn't going to tell him. He waited until he was sure she wasn't going to reply, then he firmly took her arm and escorted her inside.

He hadn't expected her home to be clean and orderly. It was crammed, as he knew it would be, with unfortunate animals, including a three-legged dog and a huge gray cat with one blind eye. He could see in one of the cages a furry back, probably of a raccoon or opossum.

Interspersed with the menagerie of animals were odds and ends she had no doubt found along the highway or that her friend Bill Garr had given her. Among her treasures he spotted a large, cracked conch shell, a statue of Venus with more than the arms missing, an old brass lamp, the base bent and dented.

"Why are you watching Lex?"

"He's got Pedro. I heard him telling Bill Garr Pedro ought to be buried with the Shoshones. But I don't want him buried. I want to look after him."

"But going home to his own people, wouldn't that make

Pedro happy?" McQuede couldn't believe he'd said that, but Roma responded as if he were making perfect sense.

"No. I'm supposed to look after him. Pedro knows that."

McQuede walked over to a huge cage in the center of the room. A rough-looking old crow with a drooping right wing peered out at him. He might be hated by farmers, gardeners, and less aggressive birds, but in Roma's house he merited a place of honor. "You've got to promise me you won't keep looking for Pedro."

"I promised Bill Garr I'd look after him," she said in a sad, singsong voice, "so I can't promise you that I won't."

Lex had been right. McQuede felt a sudden fear for her. He had to make her change her mind, to keep far away from this crime. On impulse he told her what he had asked Terese not to share with anyone. "We have found Pedro," he stated. "You don't need to look for him any longer."

"Where is he?"

"He'll be taken to Washington, D.C."

Roma looked at him, eyes widening, as if he'd just thrown the crippled crow to the cat. "What will happen to him there?" she asked despairingly.

"He'll get good care, so you don't have to worry."

Her small, pixie features puckered into a frown. "Pedro won't like it there. He's always been here."

He had no experience talking to a person who believed long-dead beings possessed feelings and rights. "He doesn't need to be cared for any longer," he said before he left.

Sid met him at the entrance to the sheriff's department. "Talbot's just made bail."

"That didn't take long."

"His big-shot lawyer's left, but Talbot's been waiting— says he's not leaving here until he talks to you."

Spotting McQuede, Talbot sprang from the bench near Sid's desk. "I told you I wouldn't spend an hour in your crummy little jail," Talbot said triumphantly.

"I do my work," McQuede drawled, "and the process goes forward." McQuede started past him toward his office.

"Is that right?" Talbot countered. "Wait and see. 'Process,'" he sputtered. "I'm going to bury you in the 'process'!"

"You'd better go about gathering your shovel, then," McQuede returned.

Talbot's spiteful words rang around him. "You'll soon see what I can do! You've made a big mistake, McQuede, the biggest mistake of your career."

Chapter Ten

McQuede sensed that something was wrong the moment he entered the Mom and Pop Café. Coal County's celebrities, Fredrick Preston III, banker and heir apparent to the Preston Mine, and his wife, state senator Heather Kenwell Preston, had stopped their happy chattering to stare at him as if he were an alien invader from some evil planet.

Ever since he'd solved the Slade case, these two had been his top supporters. He waved and said, "Good morning," noting how Heather turned away. Fredrick Preston wiped a napkin across his pencil-thin mustache and muttered a greeting so low and muffled, McQuede could barely hear him. He had planned to stop and chat with them. Instead he lifted the newspaper from the counter and settled into his usual booth. He opened the *Durmont Daily*.

TALBOT CHARGED WITH THEFT
World-famous archaeologist Dr. Seth Talbot, author of Whispers of the Stones, *claims he has been falsely charged in connection with the theft of the Pedro*

Mummy, an important artifact owned by local dealer Bill Garr, who was found dead in his shop on October 3.

"I know nothing of how this object came to be in the trunk of my car," Talbot stated. "I assert that it was planted. My belief is that there is a conspiracy that involves members of the Smithsonian archaeology team headed by Dr. Arden Reed and extends to the local sheriff's department."

The article continued on page three, but McQuede's disbelieving gaze locked on the bold, black headline in the left column.

MCQUEDE INVESTIGATED FOR BRIBERY

Dr. Seth Talbot alleged that Sheriff Jeff McQuede accepted bribe money while investigating the death and robbery of local antiques dealer Bill Garr. Dr. Talbot claims he possesses incriminating evidence in the form of a recorded conversation between McQuede and himself. He has notified the Wyoming Division of Criminal Investigation, where an unnamed official contacted by the Durmont Daily *stated that the state agency plans to follow up on these accusations.*

Talbot's revenge! Lies—articles that focused on Talbot's innocence, columns filled with half-truths and insinuations that implied, without really stating outright, that McQuede was without doubt guilty, that he had conspired with Arden Reed to frame Dr. Talbot and line his own pockets in the process.

The law would not listen to rumor and innuendo, but the local press was a different matter entirely. That was why

Talbot had wasted no time running to the newspaper with his story in a mean-spirited attempt to make good on his promise to destroy McQuede.

Although he had not looked up from the *Durmont Daily,* McQuede was aware of the Prestons' quick departure. He had never before seen a campaign ad on the front page of a newspaper, and the caption, *Vote for Integrity—Vote Don Reynolds for Coal County Sheriff,* seemed the final blow. McQuede gazed narrowly at his opponent's printed face— the big, buggy eyes, the flabby chin, the large lips that seemed to always be spouting nonsense.

McQuede prided himself on fair play, and now he was being tried and convicted by the media. Since Aunt Mattie had sold the paper, the *Durmont Daily* had made it a point to favor big-money people. McQuede dreaded the thought of a brownnoser like Reynolds taking over his job. Talk about conspiracy! Reynolds and the newspaper office had already figured out a way to defeat McQuede in the upcoming election.

He tossed the paper aside.

Katie Jones, whom everyone simply called Mom, scurried from the kitchen. She stopped to lift the coffeepot and headed toward his booth. "Now, Jeff," she said comfortingly, "no one's going to believe you're involved in this. The people of Coal County hold you in the highest esteem, and why wouldn't they? Look at all you've done for us."

"Thanks for your vote of confidence," he said gloomily. "It's probably the only one I'll get."

"Now, don't you be giving up." Mom lifted her red-checkered apron and used it to push the graying hair away from her moist forehead. The gesture seemed one of exasperation, yet her words remained staunch, "The Jeff McQuede I know is a fighter! You're not battling for yourself, Jeff, but for Coal County!" She filled his mug. "I'll just bring you a stack of hotcakes, on the house. That's going to make you feel much better."

"I'm not hungry," he replied. "The coffee will do."

Mom had intended to seat herself and have one of those long talks with him, but whoever had stepped through the door caused her to change her mind.

McQuede glanced around to see Loris crossing the room to his booth. She slipped into the bench opposite him. Mom left them alone.

"I'm surprised you want to be associated with me. You must not have read the morning paper."

"Jeff, I did read it." Loris reached across the table to touch his hand. "You know I'd never doubt you."

Relief flooded through him. When he needed her most, Loris was right there by his side, as if Arden Reed had never shown up on the scene.

"This is so unfair!"

The bells at the café entrance jingled, and Arden Reed suddenly appeared. He looked around as if searching for someone; then his gaze settled on Loris. McQuede noticed how Loris's hand left his own and settled in her lap as Reed bypassed tables to join them.

Realization washed over McQuede—Loris and Reed had planned to meet here this morning.

"I can't believe Talbot had the nerve to go to the papers like this," Arden Reed said angrily. Loris slid over, and he seated himself beside her. "Talbot's made fools of both of us!"

"I didn't think the *Durmont Daily* would allow his accusations to go public like this," Loris stated. "Were either of you contacted for a comment?"

"I certainly wasn't," Reed answered.

"Talbot was careful to make allegations only," McQuede explained. "However unfounded they are, he has a right to be heard."

"He's done irreparable damage to our project," Reed returned shortly.

No mention of the damage to McQuede's career.

"What are we going to do?" Loris broke in.

"The Smithsonian is sending accountants to audit the books and to investigate Talbot's charges. That's the first hurdle. After that, who knows? I may be fast sinking into obscurity."

Reed was gazing deeply into Loris' eyes, sparking the sympathy he wanted. To McQuede he suddenly seemed smooth and slippery with handsome, well-defined features and the gray at the temples of his coal black hair.

In the heat of his initial anger, McQuede had assumed Talbot had acted simply out of spite. His first impression began to alter. Talbot had gone to great lengths to retaliate, more than petty revenge would justify. As McQuede stared at Reed, he recalled the shocked look on Talbot's face when he had found the mummy in his car. Even though he was totally wrong about McQuede's involvement, what if he was right about Reed?

"I have a question. Ganion told me you didn't bring the Land Cruiser in for repairs until morning. Why didn't you meet Loris at the Lost Cave?"

Reed, taken aback by the abrupt change of subject, replied, "He didn't have an open appointment, so I decided to spend the day at my little apartment on Spruce. I was catching up with book work."

Or busy making another set of papers for the Smithsonian to examine. McQuede leaned back against the booth. "I keep thinking, Talbot may actually believe the story he told the paper. The mummy could have been planted in his car."

Loris gasped. "You can't really be saying that, Jeff."

"I've been defending the sheriff," Reed told her, his voice growing cold, "and he's accusing me."

McQuede didn't back down, in spite of Loris' warning look. "Talbot's being framed is a possibility I can't ignore."

Reed's entire demeanor changed, the way it had during his clash with Talbot at the museum. Loris placed a restraining hand on his arm and took up the battle for him.

"Isn't it bad enough what Talbot has done? And now you're trying to incriminate Arden? I can't believe you would do this. You two should be working together, not against each other."

"It's all right," Reed said, attempting to bring the usual mildness back into his words. "He's just doing his job."

For as long as he had it, McQuede thought ruefully. He rose, leaving money on the table for his coffee, and left the café. Loris didn't call him back or even bother to say good-bye. Obviously, she had chosen. She might feel sorry for him, but her real concern was for Arden Reed.

McQuede glanced longingly at the wrapped sandwich on his desk. Sid's noon delivery. He had thought the newspaper and his meeting with Loris and Reed had permanently squelched his appetite and was surprised to feel pangs of hunger.

He had made time over his lunch hour to meet with Ruger, who, surprisingly, had called for an appointment but would not give a hint of why, only saying, "It's urgent." It must be of the utmost importance, for Ruger generally avoided the sheriff's office like the plague.

Ruger sauntered into his office right on time, a big smile on his face. "I read all about you in the paper." He looked at

McQuede as if he had gained a whole new respect for him. Apparently, the rumors that McQuede had been accepting bribes had made him go up a notch or two in Ruger's estimation. Ruger draped himself casually into the chair opposite McQuede's desk. He took off his cowboy hat and propped it on his knee. His straw-colored hair fell in careless disarray across his forehead.

"Why call for this special meeting? Do you have some information on the case?"

"We have to discuss," again he stressed, "a most *urgent* matter."

"Pertaining to Bill Garr's death?"

Ruger kept a noncommittal silence.

McQuede lifted the ham and rye. "It's been hectic around here. Mind if I eat while we talk?"

Ruger shrugged. "Suit yourself."

McQuede had paperwork stacked to the sky and a scandal to deal with on top of an unsolved murder case. And now he'd have to handle whatever Ruger was about to dump on his plate. He hoped for once Ruger had something worthwhile to tell him. Maybe he had heard some vital bit of information from one of the dealers about Garr's murder. Whatever it was, Ruger would be sure to work it to his advantage.

McQuede began to unwrap the sandwich. "I saw you and Cory Coleman in the restaurant the other day. Mind telling me what you were arguing about?"

"Cory wanted me to buy that stuff his uncle left him."

"You didn't sound very interested."

Ruger shrugged. "I might have been if he hadn't picked out all the good items first. Guess he learned something from 'Bartering Bill' after all. Cory was trying to take me for a fool. Everything of any value was gone."

"Have you heard any rumors that Cory might have taken that mummy, either before or after his uncle's death? Maybe sold it to someone?"

"No, but I wouldn't put it past him."

"Have you had a chance to talk to that friend of Garr's, the dealer you were telling me about?"

"Not yet. But I'm sure Jonas Finney could give you some important information, if he had a mind to. He and Bartering Bill did scads of business over the years. I'll be going to Cody soon, so I'll just check him out for you."

Ruger lifted the paperweight from McQuede's desk and began to absently turn it in his hand, making the trapped colored sand shift. McQuede felt annoyed. He didn't like anyone toying with his paperweight. "McQuede, have you ever been in love?"

McQuede nearly choked on a hunk of rye bread.

Had he carved time out of his busy schedule to discuss Ruger's love life?

"Don't ask me to solve your romance problems," McQuede said gruffly. "Got enough of my own. Why are you bothering me with this nonsense, anyway? Why not ask your pal, Sammy?"

"Because you're the expert." He gazed at McQuede as if he were some kind of advice columnist for the lovelorn instead of the county sheriff, his nemesis, the archenemy who had thrown him in jail on numerous occasions.

"I mean, one-night stands are one thing. But this gal is a nice girl." He said the word *nice* as if it were a foreign concept to him. "So how do I win her over?"

First Barry Dawson asking him for advice, now Ruger. If he did lose his sheriff's election, maybe he could get his own column at the newspaper.

McQuede watched Ruger's face, looking for some sign of a

joke, but the man remained deadly serious. The impossible had happened. Cold, dispassionate, self-serving Ruger—Ruger, who had so little regard for man or beast—had fallen head over heels in love.

Who would Ruger fall in love with, and what woman would be unfortunate enough to return his affections? "So who's the lucky lady?"

"Someone we both know well."

McQuede felt a clenching in his stomach. "Wait a minute, who are we talking about here? You're not referring to . . ."

"Darcie McQuede."

"My cousin?" McQuede shot back aggressively. An image of the shy, sweet girl with her shining brown hair and sunny smile filled his mind.

Why did everyone seem to pick to love the one soul in the world most likely to make them miserable? It must be human nature that made people seek out someone totally wrong for them and believe that winning them was going to make them happy.

Visions entered McQuede's head, unpleasant visions of a wedding ceremony, of him as best man, of the preacher saying, "Ruger, do you take this woman to be your lawfully wedded wife?"

McQuede studied Ruger, speechless. McQuede sure didn't want to see him at his family reunions.

Ruger watched him like a love-struck teenager, as if his future happiness depended upon McQuede's sage advice.

McQuede cleared his throat. "Your charm will only go so far. If you want a decent woman, you are going to have to clean up your act. Darcie's not going to like your ways. She's not the type to hang out at The Drifter."

Looking lost, Ruger seemed eager to cling to every word.

"You want my advice?" McQuede boomed. "Here it is. Stay away from her! I don't want to find you anywhere near her." His outrage waned a little, and he qualified, "Darcie's an innocent girl, all lace and flowers."

Ruger's eyes lit up. "Flowers, you say? Roses! You're a lifesaver, McQuede! I'm forever in your debt."

Afternoon rounds completed, the sheriff returned to his office to find two men in dark suits waiting. They waited like statues, so sober and unsmiling, he would have taken them for IRS agents.

"We're from the Wyoming Division of Criminal Investigation," the taller of the two men said, placing a card on McQuede's desk. His closely cropped hair accentuated piercing black eyes that seemed designed for coercing confessions.

His partner, short and balding, appeared no less intimidating. "We want you to listen to this." As he spoke, he brought out a small tape recorder and placed it on McQuede's desk. He pressed a button, and McQuede recognized his private conversation with Seth Talbot in his office at the museum. Only it hadn't turned out to be so private, after all. Talbot had taped every word.

"You're on Arden Reed's payroll!" Talbot accused.

No response from McQuede, no denial.

"What do you get paid, McQuede? I know a small-town sheriff like you would leap at the chance to earn some big money."

McQuede cringed at the sound of his own dry laugh—out of context, it sounded cynical and greedy. "Money does come in handy, doesn't it? Look what it's bought you."

"So there, you admit it!" Talbot's voice rose in triumph.

More silence on McQuede's part; then the tape abruptly clicked off.

The taller of the men leaned forward, his gaze honing in on McQuede like a deadly laser. "So we'd like to know, what has the money bought *you,* Sheriff McQuede?"

"No bribery occurred. This is a weak attempt by Talbot to throw suspicion off himself."

Clearly Talbot had not planned in advance to tape him, for he had not known McQuede would pay him a visit. It followed that McQuede had fallen into a trap set for Arden Reed. Talbot had been taping their conversations, hoping something Reed would say could be used to his advantage. After Reed had left, Talbot had simply left the recorder running.

When McQuede had unexpectedly appeared, he had changed his tactics, carefully wording questions to make McQuede seem guilty of some conspiracy.

"Is that all you have?" McQuede asked. "What I hear on this tape is Talbot putting words into my mouth."

McQuede realized that he was sounding every bit as defensive as Seth Talbot when the mummy was discovered in his car. "Where's the proof that I accepted bribe money?"

His question remained unanswered. The two men watched him stonily. He cautioned himself against going on, for every word he spoke seemed to be adding to their suspicions.

"I was taped without my knowledge or permission. I have never confessed to taking any money. Moreover, this so-called evidence is not even admissible in a court of law."

"Don't forget, we have Talbot's testimony in addition to this. He claims that he overheard you plotting with Reed. He's a very respected source whose word will not be taken lightly."

"You have nothing."

"We're on your trail, McQuede." Their laser eyes bored into him. "Consider yourself under investigation."

After the two men had left, McQuede sat at his desk, turning his beloved paperweight in his hand, but the shifting, colored sands for once failed to calm him.

The shrill jangling of the phone interrupted his moody silence. What else could go wrong? He picked it up on the second ring.

"We've got big trouble down at the coroner's office," Sid told him. "A break-in. Terese Deveau's been attacked."

"How bad is it? Is she seriously injured?"

"I can't tell you. They just took her away in an ambulance." Sid paused, as if he didn't want to add to McQuede's problems. "The little Pedro Mummy's gone too," he blurted out. "It's been stolen."

Chapter Eleven

McQuede stood on the steps of the coroner's office staring at the campaign poster that now hung lopsided beneath the DURMONT CITY LIMITS sign. Someone had spray-painted a huge black X across the photo of McQuede's face. He made no move to destroy the clear-cut message, just regarded it solemnly, thinking of how little time he had left in office and wondering why he even wanted to solve this case.

Traffic had drawn to a stop, waiting while heavy train cars loaded with coal rumbled by. The long line slowly began inching forward, and as a van passed him, he came face-to-face with Roma Fielding.

She hovered in the alley across the street, where she had a direct view of the coroner's office. When she saw him, she stopped, frozen, her eyes wild and challenging.

Roma had been lurking from a safe distance, keeping watch, just as she had done at Cory's ranch and at Lex Wisken's cabin.

He had made a grave mistake telling Roma that the mummy had been found. He should have known just how she would react. If she had stolen the Pedro Mummy herself, then Roma had returned, just as she had done after attacking McQuede, to see how badly Terese was injured. Or else she was a major witness with full knowledge of who had entered and left the coroner's office.

McQuede dodged around slow-moving vehicles toward her. Once on the other side of the street, he purposely kept an even pace, trying not to alarm her. In spite of this, with the quickness of a deer in flight, Roma whirled and ran.

Halfway through the alley, McQuede caught up with her. She struggled frantically against his attempts to restrain her, just as she had during their battle near Garr's shed. But this time McQuede was prepared for each uncanny surge of strength.

"What are you doing here?"

She didn't tell him she was searching for Pedro, but he already knew that.

"How long have you been watching that office?"

Her pixielike features tightened in opposition.

He was not going to be able to force any information from her. He decided on a different tactic. "Pedro's in danger," he said. "He's been stolen again. I'm trying to find out who took him, and I'll need your help."

"I can't help you," Roma began crying. "I don't know where he is. I can't help you."

"While you were here, you saw everyone who entered the building. I need for you to name them or describe them to me."

"Just one person. A pretty woman."

"That's the anthropologist, Terese Deveau," he replied. "Was anyone following her?"

"I didn't see anyone." Roma started sobbing again. "Poor Pedro. I've got to find him."

"The woman you saw is in the hospital now. The person who stole Pedro is a killer. You've got to listen to me, Roma; you must stay out of this. I'll find Pedro. You just go on home."

Just to make sure she did, McQuede called his deputy. "I think we need to keep a watch on her."

Barry Dawson sat alone in the hospital waiting room, the way he had many years ago during his wife's final illness. Same as then, McQuede felt unable to supply the appropriate words of comfort. He merely seated himself beside Dawson, asking quietly, "How is she?"

"Too soon to tell," he replied in a worried tone. "The doctor says she may have a concussion. She'll be staying here at least overnight."

McQuede felt sure that Dawson would be here too. He cast the professor a sideways glance, wondering why from time to time he had doubted him. Their association went back many years, and he had never known Dawson to be other than ethical and responsible.

Dawson took McQuede's close scrutiny for accusation and lamented, "I know, I should have protected her."

"You couldn't have expected this to happen."

"Did this . . . maniac . . . leave fingerprints? Is there any way you can trace him?"

"The door handles and everything else he touched were wiped clean."

"Did the room show signs of a struggle?"

"Nothing was out of place," McQuede replied. "Her assailant must have entered during office hours and hidden, lying in wait for the perfect chance to steal the mummy."

Dawson's aristocratic features had become pallid. His white skin against his gray hair made his face seem carved of alabaster.

"We found bloodstains on the door frame of the lab office," McQuede went on. "Smears were on the phone and on the floor where she fell. We're running tests on the blood now, but it's sure to be hers."

As if the mention of blood was too much for him, Dawson rose and paced around the room.

"When you told me about that attack on Cory Coleman, at first I thought, for some reason or other, it might have been staged," Dawson said. "Maybe so you wouldn't consider him a suspect in his grandfather's death."

"The same thing occurred to me."

"I've been having some second thoughts. No one could say Terese is faking her injuries. Such a vicious assault. Both of them attacked in the same cowardly way." Dawson paced some more. When he turned back to McQuede, his eyes had become darker, contrasting with his paleness. "Talbot did this!"

"You can't be sure of that."

Dawson responded bitterly, "He didn't care whether he killed Terese or not. He just wanted to get his greedy hands on that mummy."

McQuede had specifically asked Terese to keep all mention of her task a secret.

"He stole it once, then the minute he gets out on bail, he steals it again!"

"How did you know the mummy had been found?"

"Terese told me." Dawson waved his hand. "Of course, she trusts me." He went on defensively, "Terese is good where security is concerned. I wanted to at least take a look at the two X-rays, but she wouldn't allow it. I'm sorry about that. If I had been there, this never would have—" Dawson stopped midsentence, in deference to the tall, stoop-shouldered doctor who had just entered the room.

"She's going to be all right," he said, but his face remained grim. "I'm going to let you see her, Professor Dawson, but she's been through a lot. Don't stay too long."

McQuede placed a restraining hand on Dawson's shoulder. "Let me ask her a few questions first."

"Is that all right with you, Dr. Ames?" Dawson asked.

The doctor glanced from Dawson to McQuede. "Just keep your questions to a minimum, and try not to upset her."

McQuede entered the room, quietly closing the door behind him. Despite the trauma Terese had experienced, her amber eyes looked clear. Purplish-blue discoloration showed beneath the bandage at her temple, trailing downward to her cheekbone.

"I need information, Terese," he said gently.

"I wish I had something to tell you." She brought her hand to her temple as if to lessen the pain. "I didn't even get a glimpse of him."

"How did it happen?"

"I was preparing to leave and had gone into the office to file some papers. I was returning to the lab when he struck me from behind."

She closed her eyes a moment, and McQuede waited for her to go on.

"He hit me so hard, like steel crushing into the side of my head."

"Do you have any idea what direction he came from?"

"Behind the couch, maybe, or from the storage closet. I remember falling. When I came to, I saw all the blood."

"But you managed to get to the phone and call for help."

"Yes. I don't remember what happened after that. I just

woke up here." She lifted a long, slender hand and let it fall on the bed in a gesture of defeat. "I'm sorry, Jeff. You did your job well. I didn't. I lost the Pedro Mummy."

"Did you tell anyone besides Dawson that it had been found?"

"No one knew but Barry and me."

With one exception, McQuede thought ruefully, the person he had told himself: Roma Fielding.

He met Dawson in the hallway, where he was impatiently waiting to see Terese.

"I'd avoid the lobby if I were you," Dawson said in an undertone. "Reed's in there, and he's in one heck of an uproar."

When Arden Reed spotted McQuede, he rose from his chair. He spoke with the same anger he'd used when addressing Seth Talbot. "I just heard about what happened to Terese." He pointed a finger at McQuede. "I've got lots of questions for you. Why wasn't I notified when the mummy was found? I should have been in charge of the examination. The Pedro Mummy falls under the archeological realm and is directly related to my project. So, what do you do? You bypass me and confide in my employee. I want to know why I was left out!"

McQuede had never been certain that Talbot's accusations concerning Reed were all based on lies, but he could hardly share that fact with him.

"I demand an explanation!"

"It has to do with your being a suspect," McQuede returned calmly.

"You're under investigation yourself. If no one's fired you, you should at least have the decency to resign."

McQuede, overlooking this acid statement, countered, "I

can hardly make you my confidant when Talbot claims you set him up."

"With your help, don't forget."

"Have you talked to Talbot since he made bail?"

"When I fired him, he left the museum in a huff. That's the last I saw of him and the last I ever hope to see."

"Then he didn't return to the museum to gather his personal belongings?"

"He's steered clear of the museum for fear of running into me. But I'm under no illusion that he will stay away from Lost Cave."

McQuede thought of the shadowy form on the cliff, the smashed car window, the deep, ugly slashes made in the tires. "What role does Talbot play in your project?"

"Talbot's goals have nothing to do with the exhibit. He's been working there behind my back. I would put nothing past him. He might even try to set up some fraudulent evidence to wow people with in his new book. He'd do anything at all to make himself famous. Now, your questions are over. It's my turn." Reed's dark eyes smoldered. "Why haven't you picked Talbot up again for what he just did to Terese?"

"Lack of evidence. But I'm going to find Talbot now and question him."

"You might be too late. By now, Talbot's probably left town." Arden Reed ran a hand through his gray-streaked temples. All the anger seemed to have left him, to have changed into defeated weariness. "And taken the Pedro Mummy with him."

McQuede had no problem getting the judge to issue another search warrant, and with it in hand, he headed to the Grand View Hotel. He inquired at the desk about Talbot.

"He rebooked his room yesterday morning," the reluctant young clerk told him. "I haven't seen him since."

McQuede placed the warrant in front of him. "I'll need to search his room."

The clerk selected a key, then said suspiciously, "I'll just go with you." The young man fell into a sullen silence, as if he'd read all about McQuede in the paper and distrusted his motives.

The elevator stopped at the top floor. The clerk hurried on ahead of him, knocking several times and calling, "Dr. Talbot."

"Open it," McQuede said.

Light from the window illuminated the empty room where McQuede had first met Talbot. The laptop was gone from the table where he had sat, as was the neat stack of books.

"I don't see his luggage," the clerk remarked, opening the closet. "He paid for three days. You wouldn't think he'd just leave without trying to get a refund."

But Talbot had definitely left. It looked as if the obvious had happened. Talbot had found out where the mummy had been taken, had broken into the lab, stolen it, and then skipped town.

Yet that conclusion didn't quite ring true to McQuede. It would take a lot of nerve, even for an arrogant, self-assured man like Talbot, to flee with stolen property when he was facing serious charges. Besides, Talbot was smart enough to realize he had little chance of getting away.

That meant he would be forced to hide out until he could get help and safely flee the country. Another scenario that to McQuede didn't ring true. A man like Talbot, so concerned about success and glory, would never consider vanishing into oblivion. A mummy without a book would not further his interests.

McQuede followed the clerk back down to the desk and checked the hotel registration. The form showed that Talbot had rented another car, this one a tan Ford Taurus. It wasn't parked in the hotel lot or anywhere in the vicinity. McQuede immediately put out an APB for the vehicle.

As McQuede headed toward his office, other possibilities struck him. Was Talbot trying to beat Reed to some final discovery? Or had he taken cover to work behind the scenes in a desperate attempt to extricate himself?

Both possibilities led him to one location—Lost Cave.

McQuede had from the first linked Talbot to the mysterious figure that Loris and he had seen at the site. It could be that Reed was right in thinking Talbot had been working on his own instead of for the project. If so, Talbot must have made some important discovery, one he didn't intend to share with Reed's team.

But what? According to Loris, nothing of value existed but cave drawings. Of course, Talbot could have discovered a rare one that would support his theory. If so, he might head there now, with nothing on his mind besides completing his work.

A slim possibility, but no others were open to McQuede. He swung the squad car around and headed toward Black Canyon. No cars passed him. His sense of isolation became complete once he had turned onto the road that wound upward toward the cliffs.

He drove for what seemed an endless time, listening to the slapping of his tires over the uneven surface of the old blacktop, feeling as if he were the only person left on earth.

The canyon walls soon encircled him. A brilliant sun,

too bright and yet void of warmth, gleamed overhead, re-flecting from sheer, ocher walls.

He reached the rutted road, little more than a jeep trail. The car's springs bucked and protested as he, driving much too fast, made the last leg of the journey. The road came to a dead end in front of the sign reading LOST CAVE.

McQuede wandered toward the outcropping of rock where Loris and he had spotted the man who had fled across the creek and escaped them. He climbed up the steep slope until he reached the place where the solid land narrowed and dropped straight down into the canyon.

Uneasiness gripped him—a presence of something unknown. He stood silently for a moment, thinking what a fool he was to be out here on some crazy hunch, without preparation or backup.

Shielding his eyes against the sun, he searched for signs of motion, but nothing stirred in the stillness. Far below, he could see the creek, the jumble of trees that grew nearby, their thirsty roots seeking water. Suddenly, through the thorny network of branches, a flash of metal caught the sun and glinted.

He leaned forward, eyes straining. He could just make out, beyond the creek that meandered through the valley, a solid image half-hidden by trees, one that from here had no definable shape.

Losing no time, McQuede edged around the precarious rise of rock that blocked his way. Glad to have that danger behind him, he descended into a meadow that gently sloped toward the creek. With each step, the soft gurgle of the water became louder.

McQuede found a place where boulders protruded from the water, and he jumped from one rock to another until he reached the opposite bank. He followed the winding creek toward where he had seen the glimpse of shining metal. Shielded by a copse of trees, he stopped abruptly. His guess about Talbot coming back here had paid off. Close to the stream, parked at an angle beneath overhanging branches, sat Talbot's tan Taurus.

McQuede scanned the area. Deciding that he was alone, he quickly crossed the open space to the car. He peered in through the driver-seat window. Nothing inside. The car was not locked, but neither were the keys in the ignition. He walked around to the back of the Taurus, wondering about the possibility of finding the missing mummy once again in the trunk. That, of course, wasn't logical—Talbot wouldn't be brazen enough to risk keeping it with him a second time. By now, he would have sent it off or hidden it, the same way he must have spirited away Arden's important research.

A sense of apprehension prompted him to return to the cover of trees. Talbot had probably spotted him already. That Talbot could be waiting somewhere above him put McQuede at a disadvantage. If he had been the one to sneak up on Garr, on Cory, on Terese, he would think nothing of lying in wait, ready to launch another brutal ambush. A cornered animal, ready to attack.

McQuede looked up at the long, steep climb he must make to the cave, and the warning voice inside him grew stronger. Foolish to go on, but crucial that he find out why Talbot was there.

Resolutely McQuede cut back across the creek, then up the slope that would lead to the stone carvings. He walked swiftly, whenever possible ducking into trees or behind shields of stone to catch his breath.

Finally he reached the first petroglyph site. He barely took notice of the faint images of animals and winged crea-tures that Loris had pointed out to him. The cave Loris had guided the way to loomed high above him, and that's where Talbot was certain to be.

He started the steep climb. He progressed slowly, using both hands to pull himself up. He tried not to think of what a bad position he would find himself in were Talbot to suddenly appear above him. Relief filled him once he had inched his way to the top and set foot on level ground.

The light was dim inside the cave. He could barely make out the carvings that Loris had called scratch-style, the more recent ones, but her definition of *recent* covered the last two thousand years.

A few cautious steps into the cave prompted McQuede to reach for his flashlight; at the moment it was of more use to him than a gun. The beam illuminated the image of *Pa waip*, the spirit who lured men into the water to drown. The thought flashed through his mind that Loris would be pleased with him for remembering that.

All the time expecting an attack, McQuede kept his free hand resting on the butt of his gun. He took a few more steps, then stopped, motionless. A faint flutter, like the motion of bat's wings, came from the depth of the cave. He waited a while, listening intently, then walked on. Soon he would reach the very end, where the tiny, eerie skeleton-like shapes carrying spears and bows were carved into the stone.

He could see them clearly now, the tiny, menacing warriors poised as if for battle. He played the light around, returning it with a jolt to the floor beneath the crude figures. The light fell across an outstretched arm with an expensive wristwatch. He knew even before he saw the initials on the gold, monogrammed ring whose bold s.t. caught the glare of his flashlight that he had found Seth Talbot.

He stepped closer, staring with disbelief at the large form clad in tan trousers and heavy forest-green sweater. Talbot lay facedown, head turned to the side, blood matting his bristly beard and forming a dark pool beneath his head.

The diminutive warriors above him seemed to be watching with open hostility. With a sick feeling in the pit of his stomach, McQuede knelt beside the body.

He had expected Talbot to have been bludgeoned like the others, but the single bullet hole told a different story. Talbot had been shot once, cleanly and at close range, through the forehead.

Chapter Twelve

McQuede handed Arden Reed the search warrant. Reed did not protest as they entered. Unlike Talbot with his fancy suite, Arden Reed had rented a small apartment on an out-of-the way street in Black Mountain Pass. Sid immediately went into the bedroom, but McQuede remained, lifting and skimming the papers on Reed's desk.

Reed watched, his handsome features stoic. He looked like a Hollywood actor, one who knew how to play the part of the suffering hero. "What do you think you're going to find by reading those? A confession?"

"Just part of a routine follow-up," McQuede replied.

"I can't believe any of this," Reed said. "My project is falling apart. First Terese is attacked, then Talbot."

"Unfortunately," McQuede drawled, "that leaves you the last one standing."

McQuede rifled through the desk drawers, then made a circle of the small room, lifting sofa cushions and inspecting the clothes in the front closet. Just as he had expected. Nothing.

He attempted to shut the closet door, but it scraped against wood and did not close. McQuede knelt to study the loose floorboards. As he began lifting them with his pocketknife, he caught a glimpse of metal.

"What did you find?" Sid asked.

"A .35 Smith and Wesson. Bag it as evidence." McQuede rose to face Reed. "This is the same caliber gun that killed Talbot. Maybe you can explain to me how it ended up here."

Reed stepped back as if the weapon had been turned on him. Dark eyebrows rose, adding great width to his eyes. Shock and surprise showed in their depths—the same reaction Talbot had had when McQuede confronted him with the mummy.

"That's not mine," Reed said with disbelief. "I've never even owned a gun."

As soon as Loris heard that McQuede had booked Reed for Talbot's murder, she charged into his office. Anger added a new, vibrant dimension that enhanced her beauty, which made McQuede wish she was here to defend him instead of Arden Reed.

McQuede tried to harden his heart. If she intended to ask for leniency, he thought with irony, she had come to the wrong man. He was committed to following the law, not his personal feelings.

"You can't believe Arden had anything to do with this! How can you throw him in jail like a common criminal?"

"Don't worry about him," McQuede said with a touch of bitterness. Reed had probably contacted the same arrogant lawyer Seth Talbot had called. "He won't spend that much time in here."

"Being released won't clear his name. Think of what this will do to his career, to our project."

"I can't ignore the facts. The murder weapon was found in his apartment."

"Were his prints on it?"

"The weapon had been wiped clean," McQuede replied. He felt suddenly weary. His personal dislike for Reed, the man who was trying to take Loris from him, did not squelch his own doubts. Finding that gun had been all too easy. As much as he wanted to tie this case up in a neat little package, he knew he wasn't yet finished with the investigation.

"What you're doing isn't right, and you know it. Someone planted that gun. Arden is being framed." Loris' eyes met his, hers bright with accusation. "He's no more guilty of this than you are of accepting bribes."

She might think McQuede could handle his own problems, but all the same, Loris hadn't taken up arms for him the way she was doing for Reed. His being in second position stung. "What do you want me to do? Overlook evidence? It's no secret Reed was angry with Talbot over that research he accused him of stealing. I even heard him say he was going to take matters into his own hands. And what about Talbot's article in the paper naming Reed as the one who had set him up? Add those to the gun hidden in his apartment, and that equals an arrest."

"I thought you would help me prove he's innocent." She tossed back her head angrily. "I have to question your motives, Jeff. You're letting jealousy get in the way of common sense and reason."

"You're talking about common sense? Where's yours? Don't you realize that there's nothing I wouldn't do for you . . . if it were possible?" He closed the space between them. "You know how much I love you." Before he could stop himself, he drew Loris into his arms and kissed her.

She responded only by slipping away from him. She gazed at him for a moment, then without another word hurried from the office.

Loris had not reacted in the way he'd hoped. His words and that kiss had only made matters worse.

McQuede lifted Talbot's book, *Whispers of the Stones,* from the bookcase where he had tossed it after purchasing it. He let the pages fall open at random, hoping that some clue to Talbot's death would jump out from the printed page.

Certain places such as the Medicine Wheel are known among the Native Americans for their magic and medicine. The local caves in Black Mountain were often used by the Shoshone and neighboring Arapaho for vision quests. Stone murals of men and animals and spirits were sought out as places of power. These locations are considered poha kahni, *or sacred.*

McQuede turned to a chapter devoted to the Little People.

Black Mountain has long been associated with magic and tales of the Nimerigar. The Nimerigar, or Little People, were believed by some to live in caves and underground passages.

Talbot's statement paved the way for his next book, which would set forth the premise that the Little People actually had existed. Talbot had joined Reed's project to bolster his theory, and likely for the same reason, had stolen years of Reed's personal research, his recordings of interviews from the local Shoshones. By making use of the project's information, Talbot might have beaten Reed to some startling new discovery. The idea that Reed and Talbot were rivals for some new find served to incriminate Reed even more.

A sharp rap on the door interrupted his reading. Aunt Mattie, as grim and as angry as Loris had been, swished into the room. As a boy he'd had trouble facing her disappointment in him—those times he'd failed to deliver a newspaper or had gotten complaints from some of her crotchety friends. The years hadn't changed that; he held his breath, preparing himself for a siege of criticism concerning those public claims that linked him with corruption and bribery. "If this is about that article . . ."

Mattie drew herself up angrily. "Yes, it is!"

McQuede did not speak, expecting to be barraged with lectures on duty and honesty.

She drew closer, slapping one of her white gloves against his desk. "Don't think for a minute I'm going to let the *Durmont Daily* get away with this. I've just finished an editorial for tomorrow's paper. That's sure to set things straight."

"You're not even going to ask me if I'm guilty?"

"Of course not!"

"Thanks for your support," he said, smiling. "It means a lot to me."

Mattie was always in a rush; he had not expected her to linger. "Jeff, it appears you were right and I was wrong."

Aunt Mattie, wrong? This time he couldn't speak.

"I actually came here because I want you to talk to Darcie. About that . . . Ruger . . . fellow." She added huffily, "He thinks he can hide his real character behind all those roses!"

"What made you change your mind about him?"

"Do you know what he did? He took Darcie to The Drifter bar!" The old Mattie had returned full force, her black eyes boring into him as if he was personally responsible. "This can't go on. She generally listens to you. You have to talk to her, Jeff. If she keeps on like this, she'll risk losing her job . . . and her reputation."

To defend Darcie's reputation, Mattie had come to someone with a worse one. Did anything make sense anymore? He didn't tell her that going to a bar wasn't the worst of crimes. He merely said, "I'll talk to her." But he knew it wasn't going to be that easy.

"You promise to do this? Right away?"

McQuede knew Aunt Mattie would give him no peace until he had honored her request. "I promise."

On his lunch hour, he walked down to the library but found it was Darcie's day off. On the sidewalk, he ran into the big-shot land investor, Bud Lambert.

"Hello, Sheriff," the man called with his usual gusto. "If you're looking for your cousin, you'll find her out at Lex Wisken's. I just came from there myself. Darcie was looking at that roan filly Lex has for sale."

"Thanks. You still trying to talk Cory and Lex into selling that land?"

"Yes, but no luck. It's too bad Bill Garr died before he had a chance to sign those papers. He told me he was fed up with both of them. He was going to cut his nephew and his so-called friend right out of his will and sell the whole lot, down to the very last acre, to me." The jolly expression vanished from Lambert's heavy face. "The way the two of them are acting now, thick as thieves . . . it just makes you wonder what . . ." His voice trailed off, leaving the rest of the sentence implied but unspoken.

Lambert began to walk away, then, noticing one of the vandalized posters, swung back. "Tough campaign, eh?" Diplomatically, he added with a big smile, "I want you to know, you've still got my vote."

The vote, McQuede thought, of a cheat and a swindler. No

doubt Lambert would be saying the same thing to the sheriff's opponent, Don Reynolds, if he were standing in McQuede's place.

Before heading out to Lex's ranch, McQuede stopped by Nate's Trading Post. What little he knew of the Shoshone legends, he'd learned from Nate. Maybe Nate could tell him more about the research Reed claimed Talbot had stolen.

He came face-to-face with Ruger, who was on his way out, happy, no doubt, because he had closed a deal. He thought about collaring him about Darcie but quickly acknowledged that any appeal to him would be useless.

"Lucky I ran into you. Just the man I wanted to see!" Ruger regarded McQuede, a devilish light in his eyes. "That is, if you're still on the case about that missing mummy."

"Why wouldn't I be?"

"With all I read in the paper"—Ruger shrugged—"I thought they might have dumped you by now."

"Innocent until proven guilty," McQuede said.

Ruger tilted his head to one side. "Isn't that my line?"

"What do you have to tell me?"

"I took a little trip to Cody and looked up that dealer, Jonas Finney." Ruger drew out the story, now that he had McQuede's undivided attention. "He wouldn't tell me much, but he knows something about that mummy. Something important. Says he might be willing to talk to you."

"Thanks," McQuede replied. "I'll check it out."

Ruger pointed his finger at him as if it were a gun. "You owe me one!"

McQuede watched Ruger head for his convertible, then entered Nate's Trading Post. No customers browsed, just Barry Dawson, seated in his usual chair. Smoke from the potbellied stove filled the air with the earthy aroma of burning wood.

"*Behne*, my friend." Nate filled McQuede's mug with coffee and handed it to him.

"How's Terese?"

"Doing fine," Dawson replied. "She was released from the hospital early this morning. What did Ruger want? He said he was going over to your office to talk to you."

"He's got some information about that missing mummy that will crack this case wide open." McQuede settled into the captain's chair, making himself the third in the usual circle. "Of course, Ruger's tips don't always pan out."

"Most of what he sells me is junk," Nate said. "But every once in a while he comes up with a treasure."

"You've had your work cut out for you lately," Dawson remarked to McQuede. Carefully avoiding any mention of the unfavorable news article, he said, "I heard you arrested Arden Reed." He paused, then added, "I spoke to him a time or two about working on the project, but Talbot rejected the idea, and in the end I wasn't hired. Reed's always so polite and mild-mannered. I never would have pegged him for a killer."

McQuede noticed how quickly even a shrewd man like Dawson accepted the idea that Reed had committed the crime, just as readily as most of the townspeople believed McQuede was guilty.

"Although if anyone could push someone over the edge," Dawson continued, "it'd be Talbot. Wonder what'll happen to the project now."

"We'll have to wait and see."

"With all the trouble that's gone on, it's just as well Talbot cut me out," Dawson remarked.

McQuede searched for signs of resentment in his tone but found none.

"Maybe they will all just leave now. The less people who

know about the site, the better," Nate said. "Those caves should be left alone, like they've been for thousands of years."

"I need a few answers, Nate. Do you think any of your people—those alive today, I mean—knew about the existence of the Lost Cave before Talbot's discovery?"

"If they did, they wouldn't tell anyone. That place is sacred." Nate thought for a moment, then added, "Lex Wisken often goes out there to seek spiritual guidance. He knows those caves like the back of his hand."

"Years ago Arden Reed interviewed some of the elders," McQuede told him, "and recorded tales about the Little People and the cave."

"I know he talked to Lex's grandmother, Mavis Wisken, right before she died," Nate said. "She had strong medicine. They say she could talk to the Little People."

"I guess I don't know much about the Native American religion."

Nate leaned forward. He looked like a leader, a wise one, black eyes glistening. He spoke in his slow way. "Our religion is not that much different from yours. Our teachers are nature. We find meaning in our relatives, in the Little People, in the deer, the eagle, and the wolf. We learn, we hear, we are connected to them. Through this union we reach out, we contact the Great Spirit."

McQuede, puzzled, said, "It's the Little People I find confusing."

Dawson explained, "That's because you think they're evil. They have a reputation for playing tricks and causing trouble, but they can also be good advisers."

"If you know how to listen," the old Shoshone said, "one may appear to you during fasting or in dreams."

"Like a spiritual guide?"

Nate nodded.

"Does Lex believe he can communicate with the spirits, then, through the Little People?"

"If so, you'll never get him to talk about it. The Little People don't like you to talk about them." McQuede couldn't tell whether Nate was joking or deadly serious. "It spoils the magic."

McQuede strode over to Lex's stables and found Darcie, who had always been crazy about horses, appraising a big shiny roan.

"What do you think, Jeff? Should I buy her? Cory says I can keep her out here. No one will care."

"She's a beauty, all right. Of course, it depends on the price."

Darcie flashed him a smile. "Cory is going to help me with the negotiations. It's so good to talk to him again. I haven't seen him since high school."

McQuede patted the horse. It whinnied softly. "Aunt Mattie's worried about you," he said. "I am, too. Ruger's just not the man you think he is."

"He's so romantic. You should see the red roses he brings me."

"He also takes you to The Drifter. Not a good place for you to hang out."

Darcie sighed. "I sometimes wish Aunt Mattie would just mind her own business."

The statement was spoken coldly and appeared to apply to him as well. He had intended to go on, share with her some of Ruger's past, but at that moment, Cory appeared. The smile on his face had changed him from the sullen-appearing person McQuede had first met to an appealing young man.

"I've saddled Run-Around," he said. "You try to keep up with me, Darcie, and we'll see how fast the roan can go."

Darcie left with Cory, leading the horse, but McQuede

remained in the stable. Cory caught hold of Darcie's hand, and through the open door their laughter drifted back to him.

"I drove her out here, and he takes over," an angry voice said.

Ruger stepped forward to stand beside McQuede, watching Cory and Darcie with narrowed, jealous eyes.

"They're old friends," McQuede said.

Ruger's lips remained compressed and silent.

"I'll be hoping that the best man wins," McQuede said lightly.

"No one is going to steal my girl."

Suddenly, as if he could bear it no longer, Ruger left the stables and strode toward Darcie. McQuede followed him.

Ignoring Cory, Ruger said to Darcie, "I have to get back to Durmont now." His voice grew colder as he addressed Cory. "She doesn't want to buy the horse."

Darcie regarded him with surprise. "I'll have to get back with you, Cory. See what Lex wants for her."

The budding love triangle, with a lot of hard looks all around, quickly dispersed. At least McQuede had fulfilled his promise to Mattie—even if in a haphazard manner that was sure to need follow-up. He started to the squad car, when he heard Lex calling to him. He was seated on one of the wooden chairs on the porch, long, jean-clad legs stretched in front of him.

"I see you and Cory Coleman are reconciling," McQuede said, settling into one of the seats beside him.

"That boy never was any good, unless he's around horses. Bill was wrong, wanting him to leave the ranch and make something of himself. He didn't know the only place he could do that is here."

"I stopped by Nate's Trading Post on the way here," McQuede said. "He told me that some time ago Arden Reed interviewed your grandmother. Said she was some kind of medicine woman."

"Grandmother lived close to the earth. But you don't have to be a Shoshone to do that. Roma also lives close to the earth. The spirits talk to her too."

McQuede knew that Lex often looked after Roma, and he could tell by the gentleness that came into his voice that he understood her in a way no one else did. "Most people think Roma's just hearing what she wants to hear, products of her imagination."

"But you believe differently?"

Lex seemed hesitant to talk. "Once there was a man who was at a crossroads in his life," he said. "Too much gambling and drinking had almost ruined him. The Little Person came to him in a dream and showed him the path he might follow, and that changed his life."

McQuede studied Lex's rough, scarred face that spoke of too much hard living and knew he was talking about himself.

"What about you? Have you ever gotten any messages from them?"

Lex's expression became somber. "It is bad luck to talk about such things."

For a while, they sat in silence, Lex watching the serene scene of rolling land, of horses and pasture. He seemed to be deep in thought, considering how much he should reveal to McQuede.

"I had a dream," Lex said finally. "In my dream the harmony was broken. Until it is restored, Roma will be in great danger."

Obviously, Lex Wisken believed he had a spiritual adviser—a Little Person—to help and guide him. If he believed Pedro's spirit resided in the mummy, Lex would be opposed to its being taken far away from the place where it was found. Realizing this led McQuede to an astonishing question: Did Lex steal the mummy from the lab?

Chapter Thirteen

Jonas Finney's store, as big a jumble of junk as Bartering Bill's, sat on a side street and occupied a huge building identical to the old warehouses that lined the railroad track. A bell jingled as McQuede entered, leaving in its wake total silence.

"Mr. Finney?"

"Back here. In my office."

McQuede dodged around tables crammed with old dishes and bric-a-brac probably scrounged either from garage sales or the city dump. From behind a desk stacked high with the same type of merchandise, a coarse chuckle sounded.

"There's a cup of coffee in it for you if you can find me."

McQuede wound through more clutter to where a bearded and whiskered old man with bright, squinty eyes and overalls sipped coffee from a chipped mug. He offered a cup to McQuede, saying, "Young fella by the name of Ruger said you might stop by. He's a slick one, good with words. Made me say I'd talk to you. But since then, I've sorta changed my mind."

"Why's that? I need your help. I'm working on an important case, the murder of Bill Garr."

The old man eyed him without comment.

McQuede sampled the coffee, so strong and bitter, it almost made him wince.

"I'm not going to be able to tell you anything," Finney concluded adamantly.

Overlooking the man's opposition, McQuede pressed on. "I understand you sold a mummy to Bill Garr about twenty years ago."

"Don't know as I recall," he said. "Too far back."

"Don't give me that, Finney. An item like that you're bound to remember."

More silence.

"The mummy you sold Garr is directly connected to this crime. Your giving me details about it is of the utmost importance." Seeing no change in his resistance, McQuede settled on a new course. "A good man who never harmed anyone was brutally murdered. I'm sure you want me to find who's responsible."

"I don't know." He eyed McQuede, rubbing a thoughtful hand through his unkempt beard. "What do you do with someone . . . if a long time ago they did something . . . you might consider criminal?"

"Don't concern yourself with that. I'm not here to prosecute you."

"Then I have your word you're not going to come back at me for anything I tell you?"

"You do." McQuede gulped the remainder of his coffee quickly and set down the mug. "Did you actually sell Bill Garr the Pedro Mummy?"

"Old Bill thought so. Until the day he died." Jonas Finney

slapped his knee and laughed as if after all these years he was still enjoying the punch line of a favorite joke.

"So you don't believe the mummy was authentic?"

"I know it wasn't." Eyes shining, Finney said, "Started out as a prank. Turned out to be the best one I've ever played."

He took another sip of coffee, then explained. "You see, Bill was obsessed with that mummy story. I told him all about it, how it had been displayed in the drugstore in Meeteetse. After that, he wanted more than anything to own the Pedro Mummy." Jonas Finney spread out rough-knuckled fingers and closed them tightly. Instead of looking at McQuede, he regarded his hand intently as if to make sure it still worked. "So, with a little help from my friend, I made his dreams come true."

"What do you mean?"

"Old Andy Schillenberg was the local taxidermist. When I told him about how crazy Bill was to find Pedro, he made him a mummy. Made it out of the bones of animals and odds and ends from his shop. Started out as just an amusement, but the end product turned out so good, we decided to sell it to Bill. You should have seen the look on Bartering Bill's face when he saw that mummy. Didn't have the heart to tell him it was a fake."

"So you let him buy it, his believing all the while it was authentic."

"You're making it sound bad, but it wasn't. We were only funnin' him. Where's the harm? Bill had what he'd always wanted, and I got five hundred dollars, which I split with Andy. That was a lot of money back in those days." Finney laughed again, the laugh ending in a hoarse cough. "We'd have told him the truth if he'd ever found us out. But that didn't happen. Never knew he'd take it so seriously. Turned out I gave him what he wanted most in all the world. He kept that mummy secret, showing it to only a select few. He was so afraid someone would steal it. Of course, rumors started that Bill owned the real thing. He got his money's worth, because everyone believed he'd bought the Pedro Mummy. And Bill thought he had, too, up until the day he died."

"Where could I find Schillenberg?"

"Andy's gone now," he said. "All my old buddies are dying off—Andy, now Bill. Only me that's left."

McQuede studied the old dealer, questioning the truth of his story. Terese Deveau had examined the mummy and had pronounced it genuine, had even shown him X-rays that compared it to the original.

Was Jonas Finney simply spinning a yarn for McQuede's benefit? From the first it had struck McQuede as strange that Ruger had gone out of his way to lead him to Finney. Ruger may have done so for reasons of his own and had made it worth Finney's while to spin a tale that wasn't true.

On the long drive back to Durmont, scenes flashed before McQuede: of Ruger and Cory arguing in the café, of the attack on Cory, of the mummy ending up in Talbot's car. A connection between those three happenings could exist. Concerning Ruger, McQuede always drew the same conclusion: There was nothing the man wouldn't do if he were offered enough money.

At least McQuede had not made the trip in vain. Whatever had taken place in Cody twenty years ago changed the way he would look at this case. He knew now he was dealing with an elaborate hoax.

McQuede had expected to hear news of Arden Reed's release, but Sid told him Reed's lawyer hadn't yet completed the process of obtaining bail. McQuede didn't ask that Reed be brought to his office; he went to the cellblock instead.

Reed rose when he saw him. The state-issued uniform hung on his slender form, yet it made him look younger, blotting out all trace of the successful, gray-suited businessman. Long, thin hands held the bars loosely. McQuede detected no hint of the arrogant hostility Talbot had shown.

"You'll be allowed to leave here soon," McQuede said. "That's why I'm here now, to caution you. You've got to stay completely out of this investigation. If you work on your own, the tables could turn on you. Do you understand what I'm saying?" McQuede stopped short, then added, "You could be in serious danger . . . if you have been framed."

"I'm surprised you consider that a possibility."

"All things are possible," McQuede returned gruffly.

"So you're suggesting I wait around doing nothing and let you handle this?"

"Exactly."

"What if I'm not so sure you have my best interests in mind?"

"I do my job," McQuede snapped. Then, feeling he'd come on too strong, he said in a milder tone, "What will happen now? To your project?"

"We're going to launch the traveling exhibit in Denver, one way or another."

"You've got lots of problems with it, for sure."

"Facing these serious charges, I'm likely to be . . . put on extended leave or even fired. You should know the fix I'm in, with all the negative publicity you've been getting."

In silence McQuede thought of his campaign posters, which had been either vandalized or had disappeared from the lawns of his prominent supporters.

"I used my one call to phone Loris," Reed told him. "The lawyer she hired for me was just in here. Loris always knows just what to do." He smiled.

McQuede was instantly riled hearing Reed talk that way about Loris, yet he forced himself not to reply. That didn't keep Reed from going on.

"Loris is so capable, possesses such ambition. She reminds me of myself when I was on my way up. That girl has a wonderful career ahead of her. She deserves all the help I can give her."

McQuede felt himself react to Reed's words, felt his body straighten, his eyes narrow.

Reed's hands tightened around the bars. "McQuede, I want you to know, I don't blame you for any of this. If I were in your shoes," he went on, "I'd have done exactly the same thing you did. With all the evidence against me, you had no choice but to arrest me."

Considering all the trouble the man was in, McQuede hadn't expected these words or the earnestness apparent in the way he spoke them. McQuede had been prepared for, and would have better been able to handle, anger and blame.

A gentleman for sure, McQuede thought. He wanted to dislike Reed but found himself holding a grudging respect for him. It even flashed before his mind that if the old adage concerning love was carried out and the best man won, it might turn out to be Arden Reed.

"I'm only hoping," Reed said, "that whoever is behind this doesn't turn out to be shrewder than both of us."

"Who is behind this? What do you think is going on? Do you have any idea?"

"I know it all centers around Seth Talbot and what prompted him to join the project. It's beginning to look as if he had an accomplice." Reed paused. "For a time, I even suspected he was working with you."

"I have trouble figuring out everyone's goal concerning

the Pedro Mummy. Talbot accused you of trying to steal his theory and his glory."

Reed gave a hollow laugh. "That childish competition was all in Talbot's head. Yes, I wanted to locate the mummy, to conduct my studies, but my reasons didn't go beyond scientific ones. I was never the least bit interested in the kind of sensational showmanship Talbot wanted. To tell you the truth, I am a reserved man who shies away from spotlights."

As much as he hated to admit it, McQuede was becoming convinced that Reed, just like him, was a victim in some complicated plot. Which put him in the position of attempting to prove innocent the man who, if free, was likely to run off with the love of his life.

"Something wrong, Sheriff?"

"No, I was just thinking. Did you ever consider the possibility that the mummy Garr had isn't the Pedro Mummy, but some clever fake?"

"It's real, all right," Reed replied with deep conviction. "Just look at all the trouble it's caused."

McQuede walked back into his office to find the two men from the Wyoming Division of Criminal Investigations standing over his deputy's desk. Sid Carlisle, looking belligerent, rose as McQuede entered. "I told them they'd have to wait for you."

"Here." The tall one with the piercing eyes thrust a paper toward him. "This gives us authorization," he snapped, "to audit the books you keep for Coal County. After that, we'll be needing to take a look at your personal accounts."

McQuede glanced at it, then back to the investigator. He hadn't gotten any friendlier since their last meeting.

"I've been reading in the paper that you arrested Arden Reed for Talbot's murder," the tall man said.

McQuede made no reply.

"Looks as if Talbot was right about all the accusations he made."

"Not all of them," McQuede returned. "If Reed did kill Talbot, there wasn't any conspiracy. I had nothing to do with it."

The inspectors exchanged smug, know-it-all glances. The bald one said, "I wonder what Talbot would say to that? Too bad he can't take back his statement from six feet underground."

Sid immediately became defensive. "Just hold on a minute. You're not talking to a criminal. Jeff McQuede is the finest sheriff Coal County's ever had. Do you want to know why? Because people trust him. While you're here, you can show some respect."

The short, balding investigator again exchanged glances with his partner, then, jerking his head toward Sid, said, "We're not going to get any assistance from him." He gave Sid a long, hard look. "But we don't need it."

"You'll get full cooperation from us." McQuede turned to Sid. "Give them full access to all of our records."

McQuede entered his office and sank down at his desk. He felt as combative as Sid appeared, but as he'd told Talbot, the process goes forward. They'd probably be underfoot for days, rifling through files, looking for traces of corruption and mismanagement. Through the glass-panel door he watched Sid lead them toward the bookkeeping division.

McQuede remained still for a while, not thinking of the case or his predicament but of Loris. He would get over losing his job, but he might never get over losing her. He reached for the phone. "Loris."

"Jeff?"

"I want to talk to you. Can you spare a minute?"

He held his breath, prepared for a rejection.

"I could take a break. Would you be able to meet me at the café in about a half hour?"

"I'll be there."

McQuede arrived early. Mom wasn't there, only her husband, whom everyone called Pop, a small, silent man who seldom looked up from his duties, not even to greet his customers. McQuede seated himself at their usual booth. In the quiet, he remembered how he had tried to gather up the courage to ask Loris out for the first time and how, at the last moment, he'd lost his nerve. By chance the very next day they had ended up here at this café, in this booth, after she had called him for help concerning a museum break-in. Although it hadn't been a real date, he had considered it one, and from that moment on he had thought of no other woman but her.

He rose as she entered and watched her walk toward him.

"Could you bring us some coffee, Pop?" he called.

Pop hurried over, placing the steaming cups in front of them.

"Arden called me," Loris said, after Pop had returned to the counter. "He's asked me to take over the project for him."

"That's a big task," McQuede muttered, jealousy returning full force.

"It's just temporary. We're hoping he'll soon be free of these charges, and he can go on to Denver as scheduled. If not, he wants me to take his place."

"He's asking a lot of you."

"Not really. Most of the hard work has been completed. We have put together more than enough material for the Denver exhibit. And the best part of it is, we won't be needing to go out to Lost Cave again."

Loris ducked her head, and strands of thick, honey-colored hair fell forward. She looked up again, sadness darkening her eyes, and she did not speak for a very long time. "Sometimes I wish none of this had ever happened. It would have been better for all of us. If I'd never accepted this assignment, if I'd never met Arden . . ."

"I wish you meant that part about Reed, but you don't, do you?"

"I guess you're right about that. Once in a while, you meet someone you know is going to change your life. That's how I felt when I first saw Arden."

McQuede remained gazing at her in solemn silence.

"He says I have great promise, great potential. He's going to promote my career."

Loris looked away from McQuede, toward Pop, who, oblivious to them, was leaning on the counter reading the newspaper.

"I never married, Jeff. I don't have children. My work is my life."

"I can't find fault with that," McQuede replied. "Your work is probably as important to you as mine is to me."

"Jeff." Loris reached across the table, her hand falling lightly on his. "I guess I depend on you way too much, your being there, your understanding."

McQuede drank his coffee, silence falling around them. After a while, he spoke. "Are you in love with Reed?" McQuede went on quickly, "Don't answer that. I don't even want to know."

Loris smiled at him. "I've told you this before, but I mean it. You really are one of the good guys, Jeff McQuede."

A good guy. A compliment, yes, but she had not answered his question.

Chapter Fourteen

There's been an accident." Cory Coleman's words over the phone ran together, muffled and distant.

"What's happened?"

"Roma's had a fall. It looks bad. You'd better hurry."

"Where are you?"

"At Lex's. I've called an ambulance, but I don't think she's going to make it until it arrives."

As McQuede sped toward Lex's cabin, tightness gripped his heart. An image of Roma's childlike large eyes seemed to watch him, to say, "You should have protected me. You've let me down."

The squad car reared in protest as wheels hit ruts. He pulled to a stop near Lex's cabin, spotting the beams of moving lights far back against the cliff. He plunged through trees and foliage, following the deep gorge toward the high ridge where not long ago McQuede had spotted Roma keeping watch on Lex. An image of Roma perched on a log, huddled in her tattered clothes, merged with the imagined sight of her small, crumpled form. He increased his pace, knowing already that speed would be of no importance. He reached the bearers of the flashlights out of breath.

Lex, a huge, dark shadow, rose and backed away from the fallen body. McQuede took his place. Roma lay as still as death, eyes closed. He leaned closer, detecting a faint, shallow breath. A deep gash sliced across the base of her skull. Because of the distant rise and fall of a siren, McQuede decided not to risk moving her head in an attempt to stop the bleeding.

Cory's voice sounded above him, still choked and hard to understand. "I was out riding, and I'm the one who found her." His words broke off, as if he were on the verge of tears. "The way she runs wild all day, I was afraid something like this was going to happen. She must have gotten too close to the ledge and slipped on a loose rock."

McQuede made no reply, but he thought Cory's explanation unlikely. Roma, as nimble as a goat, spent most of her time roaming the mountainside and knew the area well. Moreover, Roma had ignored his warning and returned to the cliff near Lex's cabin. She had to have some reason for being out here.

McQuede glanced toward Lex. In the darkness he was only an outline. He looked up at the sky, arms uplifted, imploring the powers that be to let her live. It made McQuede think of the medicine man in Frederic Remington's painting *Conjuring Back the Buffalo*.

For a moment, McQuede wanted to join him. Instead, he leaned closer to Roma. "Roma, can you hear me?"

Her eyes remained closed, but he noted the faint movement of her hand. He could barely make out her words, "Face . . . all wrapped."

"She's talking about that blasted mummy!" Cory said. "She's as obsessed with it as Uncle Bill was." He turned away, moaning, "That evil little thing will ruin us all."

Lex's deep voice, curt and sharp, overrode the last of Cory's sentence. "Don't say that."

Cory didn't answer him, just turned and started back toward the house to meet the arriving paramedics. McQuede focused his full attention again on Roma. If only she would be able to tell him what had happened. "Roma . . ."

If she lost consciousness, chances were she might never be able to speak to him again, to supply him with the answers he so much needed. No matter how cruel it seemed, he had to try again. "Roma, who did this to you?"

Once more her hand moved slightly.

Roma knew who had attacked her; if only she could tell him. McQuede tried to get some response from her again, but the clamor of the medics, Cory in the lead, squelched that hope.

McQuede moved back to stand beside Lex. He could see, from the strong lights the team from the hospital carried, the tears that flowed down Lex's face. The two of them waited quietly, side by side, as they had done outside of Bill Garr's shed.

As the stretcher passed them, Lex stepped forward. He vowed to Roma, "I will ask the spirits to help you. I will pray to them to keep you safe."

McQuede had left the hospital late that night and returned early the next day.

"Dr. Parker will be available to talk to you in about a half hour," the nurse at the desk told him.

"Will I be able to see Roma Fielding?"

"You will have to wait for the doctor."

McQuede, resigned, went into the waiting room. He had not expected to see Aunt Mattie. It took a moment for him to recall that she and Roma's mother had belonged to the same garden club.

"Any word about her condition?" he asked, seating himself beside her.

Aunt Mattie placed aside the basket of needlework she had brought with her to pass the time. "She hasn't regained consciousness. Poor child. And your poor Aunt Mattie, too. I've been here since dawn. Dear, would it be too much trouble for you to get me a cup of coffee?"

The complimentary pot was empty, so McQuede headed to the cafeteria. When he returned, Darcie was seated on a couch across from Mattie with Cory Coleman close beside her.

Cory seemed older, his lean face etched with worry and weariness. He responded to McQuede's questioning gaze. "Roma didn't have anyone to stay with her last night, so I did."

"Roma was in our class in school," Darcie added sadly.

"Uncle Bill thought a lot of her," Cory said, his voice taking on Darcie's remorse. "I've never known a time without Roma around. I guess I just took it for granted that that would never change."

"Now, don't go jumping to conclusions," Mattie said, falling back on her old proverbs for support. " 'Where there's life, there's hope.' "

Cory's gaze remained fastened on McQuede. "I met Roma earlier yesterday, when I was out riding. I don't know whether she imagined it or not, but she told me someone had been in her house."

"Was anything missing?"

Cory shook his head in a puzzled way. "What does she

have to steal? Then I got to thinking she might be right, that the same person who had broken into my place had been in hers too. I went back to her house with her."

"What did you find?"

"I couldn't see that anything was disturbed. It's hard to tell about Roma—how much you should believe, I mean. She kept saying her lamp was gone."

When McQuede was in her house, he had noticed a small lamp base fashioned from either brass or iron, bent and flawed like the stray animals that occupied her house. Likely she had found it cast aside or hidden in the woods beside the road. He wondered if it was the weapon used to murder Bill Garr, stolen from Garr's shed by the killer.

That went along with his belief that Roma had not been in any accident. The way she lurked around, seeing everything—the killer doubtlessly had reason to believe that Roma could point him out.

Cory reached for Darcie's hand, his gesture of comfort unmissed by Aunt Mattie who lifted her sewing and began rapidly plying the long needle. After a while, Mattie asked without looking up, "What sort of work do you do, Cory?"

"I'm on the verge of investing in a business," the young man replied.

"Investing is not work," Mattie said.

"But much easier," Cory replied with a small smile.

"This business, is it in Iowa? Will you be going back there when this is over?"

Cory's hand tightened on Darcie's. "It's good to be back here in Wyoming, to be working with the horses again." He cast Darcie a quick, sideways glance. "You never can tell. I may just decide to stay."

After a while, Garr's nephew addressed Mattie again.

"Not everyone finds their niche in life like you have, Mrs. Murdock. You do have a way with words. Very vivid and convincing. I read your editorial in last night's paper."

He had spoken the magic words. Mattie stopped knitting and smiled at him.

McQuede was surprised when he looked up and saw Terese Deveau. She crossed the room and stopped beside him. A blue-patterned scarf had fallen away from her face, revealing swelling and multicolored bruises. She carried a small vase of red and white carnations.

"I just dropped by to see how she's doing," she said. "I don't really know Roma, but . . ." Terese's voice trailed off. When she continued, her tone had a hollow, frightened ring, "Loris doesn't believe what happened to Roma was an accident. She thinks Roma was attacked just like me."

"We don't know that yet," McQuede replied.

Her amber eyes held his. "I haven't seen Arden Reed, but I've heard he's out of jail. I expected him to show up at the museum this morning, but he didn't."

Before McQuede could reply, the same tall, stoop-shouldered doctor he had spoken to last night appeared at the door. He stood appraising them, his expression solemn. "I'd like to talk to the family of Roma Fielding."

"She has no family," Cory said, rising. "But everyone here is concerned about her."

Dr. Ames glanced around at them again. "Her condition is grave. I'm surprised she lived through the night."

Of all things, McQuede thought of the birds and animals waiting for Roma at home. He didn't look at Darcie, who had begun to cry.

"Before Miss Fielding arrived at the hospital last night, she had lapsed into a coma," the doctor went on. "Given her injuries, she has little, if any, chance of regaining consciousness."

"Darcie and I will stay," Aunt Mattie said. "Doctors aren't always right. Things may change."

McQuede would have liked to wait with them, but he needed to question Arden Reed.

Tired, he stopped outside, lingering on the hospital steps, watching Cory Coleman start across the parking lot. Cory had almost reached his car when Ruger suddenly appeared out of nowhere to block his path.

McQuede could not make out their loud, harsh words. But he could see the deep anger in Ruger's face and the way his fists clenched.

McQuede didn't reach them in time. Ruger punched Cory, a hard blow to his face. The young man stumbled backward, caught himself against the hood of his car, and attempted to fight back. Ruger sidestepped the blow and jabbed him in the stomach. Cory doubled over in pain. Ruger stood over him menacingly.

Determined to carry on with the fight, Cory straightened.

McQuede's heart froze as he saw Ruger's hand slide beneath his vest—like a gunfighter in the Old West. McQuede knew that Ruger often kept his deadly Blackhawk concealed there. Cory knew it too. He froze motionless, his eyes widening.

McQuede lunged forward. He wrested Ruger's arm behind his back, checked for a weapon, then pushed him roughly away.

"What's going on?"

"He started it!" Cory spat out. He attempted to look tough but managed to appear only shaken and disheveled.

"You can bring assault charges against him," McQuede said.

"I don't want to do that. He's crazy! You deal with him!"

"Then get into your car and leave," McQuede ordered. "Ruger, you're coming with me."

Ruger made no protest as McQuede opened the passenger door to the squad car. McQuede headed to his office but on impulse changed his mind and swung into the drive-through restaurant behind The Drifter bar.

Ruger, showing no sign of cooling off, belligerently set aside the coffee McQuede had ordered for him. "Cory's the one who started this. You can see for yourself. He's trying to steal my girl."

"You have to win her, not eliminate him. And I told you before, you can't do it. You've already estranged her in some way, haven't you?"

"I don't know what the big deal is. I went out to The Drifter with Sherry last night, and we got a little drunk. We danced a little, had a good time. So what? Sherry and I go back a long way. Now Darcie won't even talk to me. The next thing I know, she's crying on that loser's shoulder!" Ruger lifted the coffee, finished it in one gulp, then crushed the cup in his hand. "I'll fix him! I would have before this, if I'd had my Blackhawk with me."

"See what I mean? That's the reason you don't have a chance with her. You and Darcie live in two different worlds." McQuede realized his words sounded like some old country music song, one he'd heard and should have forgotten.

They sparked even more anger in Ruger. He glowered at McQuede, eyes fire-blue. "This isn't over! I could get even. I know people."

"What does violence ever solve? It just creates a multitude

of other problems." McQuede should be hauling Ruger off to jail, not talking to him like some Dutch uncle. Maybe McQuede should cut him a little slack, because he knew how hard it was to be odd man out in a love triangle.

Talk, Ruger didn't understand—just force. McQuede decided to try that. "If Darcie ends up getting hurt, I'm not going to like it. I'll come looking for you."

"Then I'll fight you too."

"You're not going to win. Losing Darcie is the only thing that can happen here. Just let her go, like a gentleman."

"Maybe that wimp Cory might be a gentleman, but I'm not! And neither are you." Ruger's features seemed set in stone, yet his eyes still flared with deep-rooted anger. "I'm not ever going to give her up!"

Doubting the wisdom of letting Ruger go, McQuede nevertheless took him back to his car. He watched as Ruger sped out of the parking lot, then turned his attention to more crucial matters. Before he picked up Arden Reed for questioning, he must establish that Roma had not been the victim of an accident.

If the killer had left some clue, he was going to find it. He stopped first at Roma's house. He would begin here and try to follow the same course that last evening she must have taken to Lex's land.

There had been no need for any intruder to break in. The lock on the door didn't look as if it had worked for years. He stepped inside, circling the room. The three-legged cur struggled to his feet, loped after him for a while, then settled back down again beside the long-cold stove.

"You might be losing your best friend," McQuede said, patting the dog's furry head.

The animal whined as if it understood.

McQuede filled the bowls with food and water, then began to search through the rooms.

Roma had openly been looking for the mummy. Somewhere along the line, she must have come face-to-face with the murderer. He must have known that she knew all about his crimes and had come here to silence her. If McQuede were right, the missing lamp played a major role in what had happened. That's why the killer had taken it and then gone after Roma.

The walk from Roma's place to Lex's cabin must be less than a half mile. Alert to every detail, like a tracker, McQuede followed the path she had probably taken. Soon the corral came into view, where she had run across Cory. If he had gone back to her house with her, as he claimed, then she had left again, the killer on her trail.

McQuede kept to the high ridges, stopping occasionally to look down at Lex's fine stock of horses grazing in the pasture below. Today no smoke came from Lex's cabin.

McQuede soon reached the treacherous drop-off where Roma had fallen. The bank had crumbled and scattered rocks down into the ravine. But he had no way of knowing whether Roma had been involved in a struggle with someone or whether she had simply gotten too close to the edge.

Keeping careful watch for any clue, he made his slow way down the cliff, hands and feet seeking out supports sturdy enough to hold his weight. After a treacherous descent, he reached the bottom.

Blood had dried on the stone floor where Roma had lain. He searched the area, examining the rocks that had slid down with her, but he found nothing.

McQuede widened his search, stopping here and there to lift some large stone, then toss it aside. He had gotten some distance from where she had fallen and, on the verge of giving up, stopped to kick a large, jagged rock with his foot. As it rolled over, he noticed a dark discoloration. He lifted it carefully, aware that what he was seeing was dried blood.

Roma must have been running away, her assailant in fast pursuit. Whoever had been behind her had lifted this very rock and hurled it at her. He studied the jagged edge that had cut the gash into the back of Roma's head. He could almost see the stone crack against her skull, ricochet off, and crash down into the canyon with her. McQuede drew in his breath, knowing he was holding in his hand the weapon that had been used in the attack on Roma Fielding.

Chapter Fifteen

T he rock McQuede had found beneath the cliff verified the fact that Roma, too, had been attacked, yet no evidence pointed to her assailant. Because Arden Reed had been released from jail just before the mummy had been stolen, McQuede had told Sid to bring him in for questioning. But as of yet, he had not been located.

McQuede leaned back in his chair, thinking of Roma and recalling her strange expression as she had watched the lab. He thought again of the words she had told him after her fall, her last words before she lapsed into a coma: *face all wrapped.* Cory thought she had been talking about the mummy, but that didn't make sense, for Pedro had not been wrapped in bandages like an Egyptian mummy. She could simply have been hallucinating, or she could have been trying to tell him something about her and Terese's attacker.

Face all wrapped. Possibly that was in reference to a ski mask. If Roma had followed the person who had broken into the lab, believing that he had the mummy, that would account for the attack on her.

Each possible conclusion left McQuede unsure and troubled. Everything centered around the mummy. If Finney had told him the truth about the hoax he had plotted to hoodwink Garr, the mummy had been used in another, even bigger hoax. McQuede lifted his magic paperweight and slowly turned it in his hand. He concentrated on the player or players, and when the sand had settled, he had his answer.

He sat bolt upright in his chair. All along he'd been thinking just the opposite of what had happened. The theft of the Pedro Mummy wasn't the real motive for the crime, nor was it a red herring intended to draw attention away from the criminal. It was a ploy used for one purpose, to frame Seth Talbot. He would find a clue, if any existed, out at the cave Talbot had discovered.

Before leaving his office, he scribbled a note for Sid. *Gather all information available on the Pedro Mummy.*

He drove quickly, soon leaving the blacktop for the rutted road that wound toward the petroglyph site. The canyon walls appeared now to box him in, to block the possibility of retreat. The hazy peaks of the mountains merged with the dark, low clouds, making the sky seem closer, as if it, too, were closing in around him.

The downpour of early morning had ceased. Only a spattering of raindrops struck his windshield, making streaks when he turned on the wipers. By the time he reached the turnoff, the rain had stopped. Water, overflowing in places, made puddles along the deeply eroded trail. He stepped harder on the gas, car wheels sliding through deep mud.

McQuede pulled to a stop near the Lost Cave sign. With the project now in limbo, the site loomed before him, empty and abandoned. He stepped out, aware of the mingling scents of earth and pine. Mud sucked at his boots as he trudged toward the first cliff where primitive likenesses of men, elk, and bison were carved in stone.

McQuede regarded them, then looked up, anticipating with dread the long, steep climb up to the cave Talbot had discovered, the cave where he had met his death.

Droplets of water glistened from the huge, ochre-colored rocks. Knowing the recent rain had made the stones slick, with great care McQuede moved from handhold to foothold, inching his way up. By the time he reached the top level, his fingers were stiff and numb with cold. He stopped to catch his breath, to wipe damp hands across his jacket.

An ominous gray haze had settled over the canyon, making it impossible to tell exactly where the mountains ended and the sky began. He felt as if he had somehow entered another dimension, a mythical world far above the clouds.

Clicking on his flashlight, McQuede stepped through the cave's rock entrance. He stopped, playing the beam across ancient walls. The weird carvings cut deeply into the stone made the cave seem a prohibited territory, one guarded by ghostly images, all opposed to his intrusion.

His footfall resounded in the heavy silence as he made his way deeper into the darkness. At the end of the cavern, he came across an abandoned knapsack. He looked inside, found it empty except for a canteen.

Carvings decorated the solid rock in front of him and extended to the great slab to the left. To his right, the wall had long ago crumbled, leaving an eruption of boulders, many of them displaced again by archaeologists.

Here Talbot had discovered the oldest of the carvings, still figures frozen in time, ones that Talbot had hoped would be a link to the existence of the Little People. McQuede played his light around, fixing it for a moment on the place where he had found Talbot's body.

The site had not been totally cleared. Tools had been left tossed in a stack beneath large, broken stones. McQuede sifted through them. He lifted a long-handled spade, holding the light to the blade. He noticed, deeply embedded in the handle where it met the metal, a faint discoloration. Blood. Talbot had fought with someone in this very cave. This weapon had left a telltale clue.

At that moment McQuede tensed. He swung the beam toward the rocks. As he did, he got the impression of an eerie glow coming from underground. He stood for a moment, frozen. Whiffs of a familiar scent rose from the earth beneath, the smell of burning sage.

He quickly switched off his light and stood immobile. From out of the total blackness the muffled sounds of a chant rose and fell, seeming to encircle him. The volume increased like a battle cry, as if the tiny stick-figure men had come to life.

Definitely not an ancient phantom. McQuede edged closer to the faint light and the supernatural strains that continued to flow upward. Using his hands for eyes, McQuede determined the position of the stones and hoisted himself up to a large, flat rock. He could see now the jagged, gaping hole that opened into a lower chamber, one just large enough for a man to slip through.

So this underground passage was Talbot's new discovery. The research he had stolen from Reed must have contained some clue that had led him here. He had not shared his find with Reed and the team but had carefully kept it a secret.

But someone else knew about it too. McQuede knelt, peering into the opening. A lantern was set in the center of the small cave, its glow outlining a broad form with uplifted arms.

Lex Wisken! Of course, he would know about the cave

where his people had for many years gone for strength and vision—his sacred place—*poha kahni*. He had come here to ask the spirits—the Little People—for a healing for Roma.

McQuede quietly lowered himself into the small chamber. All the while Lex's chants continued. He looked larger than life, the broad shoulders, the long braid. His head was raised, eyes closed in trancelike prayer.

The lantern cast shadowy light across the unusual shapes etched into stones, much different from the ones above and likely much older. They portrayed horned figures and strange, stylized creatures. Complex symbols scattered around them that McQuede could not begin to decipher. Animals and spirit shapes, no doubt symbols of magic.

He glanced again to Lex, then back at the wall. This time his gaze locked on a dark shape perched on a small ledge of stone. He drew in his breath and stepped back, hardly able to believe his eyes. There, flanked by a background of carvings, sat the missing Pedro Mummy.

Lex, as if aware of some negative force, ceased chanting. He turned slowly to face McQuede.

"I had no idea that you . . ." McQuede began.

"I didn't take the mummy. I didn't bring it with me. I found it. I came to pray for Roma."

"Do you expect me to believe that, Lex? No one else even knows about this place."

"Grandmother took me with her many years ago to communicate with the spirits. I came to this spot for my vision quest. But it has been desecrated." The lines tightened in his broad face, making him appear immensely angry. "Sullied by profit seekers!"

Had everything McQuede put together been wrong? What if Lex had encountered Talbot here, and the blood he'd found on the spade was Talbot's?

Lex spoke again. "Roma could name the killer, and she was afraid. You think she was attacked while watching my cabin, but that's not true. The killer knew Roma could identify him and came out to silence her. She fled toward the cliffs, and he was following her. She was trying to reach me, trying to get to safety."

McQuede stared at him, no longer certain of his previous conclusions.

A slight noise broke through the vast silence, hollow and resounding, metal clanking against metal. Another person, maybe Lex's accomplice, was just above them, rummaging through the stack of tools to remove the incriminating spade.

McQuede glanced at Lex. His stony expression gave no clue to whether or not he was a co-conspirator.

McQuede had to make a snap decision. He must try to get back up to the main cave, take the person by surprise, and avoid another disaster.

"No matter what happens, Lex, you stay down here," he said, his words barely a whisper.

He could feel Lex's hard gaze on his back as he began to hoist himself up to the main part of the cave.

Whoever had entered the upper cave had set down a bright light, the kind used by archaeologists. He had to take a chance, to act quickly. Before he was able to clear the opening, he saw the gun that was aimed directly at him.

Terese Deveau's injuries had nearly healed, yet she still wore a blue patterned scarf to hide the bruising that remained—*face all wrapped.*

He pulled himself up and got to his feet.

"So you found it," she said. "Talbot's last discovery, the one he kept to himself." Anger glinted in her amber eyes. "His next book would add to his fame, to the fortune he'd already made by deceit."

"By deceiving you?"

Before responding to his question, she said in a low, threatening way, "Take that gun from your holster, and lay it on the ground."

McQuede didn't have a chance of firing it. She would shoot him dead if she even thought he was going to try. Careful to make his motions slow, he removed the gun and let it fall down into the lower chamber. A dull thud sounded as it struck the rock floor beneath them.

"Yes, by betraying me!" Terese's eyes narrowed. "I hated him! You saw the way Talbot sabotaged Arden Reed, undermining him, stealing his research. He did the very same thing to me. I was the one who discovered this cave in the first place. Seth Talbot took my find over, stole all the glory. I let him do it because at that time I thought I was in love with him. I thought we were partners for life, that we would marry and become one. After he had gotten what he wanted from me, though, he threw me over."

"Why didn't you bring suit against him?"

"I had no proof that the research was mine. He would say that I was little more than a secretary, that I was acting out of jealousy, and everyone would have believed him."

"So you hated him in silence and finally were presented with an opportunity to get even."

"I didn't intend to kill him, just to bring him down. Only to make the world stop applauding him and see him as the monster he really was!"

"So after Bill Garr contacted you, you beat Talbot to his shop. You intended to steal the mummy and blame the theft on Talbot."

"Garr caught me before I was able to leave the shed. I didn't mean to kill him. I was so scared. He began yelling at me. I just picked up that lamp base and hit him."

McQuede had been on the wrong track thinking that the killer was still looking for the mummy when Cory's house was broken into. Terese had not returned to steal anything but to plant the letter Talbot had written to Garr, knowing it would point to his guilt.

"What about Roma?"

"When I broke into Reed's apartment to plant the gun, she was outside watching me. I knew right then, she knew way too much. But I never once planned and never wanted to harm anyone."

Terese watched him, wide-eyed, the gun aimed steadily at his heart.

"Talbot didn't consider you much of a threat, but it turns out you're a match for him, after all."

"He was always afraid someone was trying to steal his glory. I went out of my way to convince him that Reed was behind this. Because I had let him get by with what he had done to me for so long, it didn't cross his mind that it was me. When he heard I was examining the mummy and my lie that it was authentic, he came to me and offered me a good deal of money if I would turn it over to him. He intended to hide it in the part of the cave no one else knew about and use it later, once he was free of the charges against him.

"I told him I would meet him here with the mummy. He was so smug, so evil. He wanted the Pedro Mummy so badly. I decided this *was* my revenge. I laughed in his face and told him it was a fake! You never saw anyone so furious. But when I turned to leave, he took me by surprise and hit me with the spade . . . so hard I believe he meant to kill me. I didn't come out here unarmed. I shot him." She straightened up. "I'm not sorry. He deserved to die."

"With your serious injury, how did you manage to make it back to the lab, much less plant the gun in Reed's apartment?"

"When you're desperate, you're often able to do what in other situations seems impossible! My last hope lay in making it look as if I was attacked at the lab and that the mummy had been stolen."

"I had thought someone was framing Talbot, but I never once thought of you, even though I knew you had worked with him and had once been a pair. You did a good job of setting Talbot up. You knew he was out at the site and would be blamed for the destruction you did to our vehicles."

"My big mistake was telling you that the mummy was authentic," she said.

"At first I never thought to doubt your examination." McQuede replied. "Not until I talked to Jonas Finney, who had sold the mummy to Garr. He swore it was a fake. That's when I realized you'd lied to me. The new X-ray of the Pedro Mummy you showed me was as fake as the mummy itself. It was simply a duplicate of the original X-ray from the fifties. The evidence is in my office right now, and that is what's going to prove your guilt."

"No one's going to make that connection but you, and you're not going to be alive to tell about it."

"Your scheme was very well plotted," McQuede said, "but I still don't know how you could have been so sure that you would be the first one to examine the mummy."

"It was easy to get Barry Dawson, an expert in forensic anthropology, to recommend me. I used the original X-rays from the Pedro Mummy to convince everyone that Bill Garr's fake was the original. I intended all along to destroy it, which I'm going to do now."

"And after you do, you intend now to take over Talbot's plan and try to prove his theory."

"In a year or two, when I'm ready, I will return and re-open the project. Then I'll announce that I've discovered another section to the cave. I will do what he planned to do—link this valuable petroglyph site with the Little People, write his book, and get rich and famous myself. It's too bad you kept pursuing this," she said with a tight smile, "Now you're going to disappear, McQuede. For the time being, I'm going to bury you and the phony mummy down in the lower chamber. You won't be found there. Except for Talbot, no one, for over two thousand years, has discovered the lower passage. Until I am able to return and dispose of your remains, you can keep Pedro company."

"That's going to be hard to do," McQuede said evenly. "I've searched the chamber from end to end. There's no mummy down there."

"It's on the ledge where I placed it after I killed Talbot."

"If you ever put it there, someone must have found it. Maybe Arden Reed."

"I don't believe you!"

"Take a look for yourself."

Terese glanced toward the gaping hole. At that instant, a shot exploded from right beneath them.

Terese let out a gasp and jumped back. At the same time, McQuede lunged toward her, yanking the weapon from her hand.

As McQuede was clamping handcuffs on Terese Deveau, Lex climbed through the opening. He quickly got to his feet and handed McQuede's gun back to him. He stared for a long, solemn while at Terese. "My prayers are answered," he said. "The killer has been delivered into our hands."

Chapter Sixteen

McQuede met Ruger in front of the Mom and Pop Café. Ruger's features held a lingering scowl of anger, although his voice remained quiet and placid, as if he had just come to terms with something important to him.

"I suppose by now you've heard. Darcie's ditched me for Cory."

McQuede found himself falling back on one of Aunt Mattie's proverbs, " 'Water seeks its own level.' Can't say I didn't warn you."

"If she wants to tie up with a jerk like him, then let her. She's not smart enough for me." Ruger paused, then added, "But I really did care about that girl."

Even though Ruger's expression remained impassive, McQuede sensed his deep remorse. This unusual glimpse of Ruger caught him off guard and sparked a touch of pity. McQuede even attempted to cheer him. "It would have been a little awkward, after all, wouldn't it? You and me at family reunions."

"You mean now we can go back to being enemies?"

Ruger grinned as if he found the idea as appealing as it was to McQuede.

"Count on it," McQuede said.

McQuede went into the café. Barry Dawson was seated alone at a back booth, and the sheriff crossed the room to join him.

"The Pedro Mummy is still missing," Dawson said remorsefully. "The one Bill Garr had was only a fake made of bits of taxidermy."

"Do you think the real Pedro Mummy will ever be found?"

"Not likely. Even though the X-rays indicate it wasn't a hoax, now no one will ever know for sure whether or not the original mummy was a deformed infant or a full-grown man, evidence of the existence of the Little People."

"Maybe it's better that way," McQuede said. "There should be some mysteries in this world that are never solved."

"What a fool I've been," Dawson lamented. "To think, I was the one who recommended that Terese examine the mummy."

"You saw what we all saw, an efficient person, someone to rely on."

"I've always prided myself on being such a good judge of character. What do you think went wrong? Why didn't I know?"

"You were hit by one of Cupid's arrows," McQuede replied. "Don't they cause total blindness?"

"And loss of judgment," Dawson added.

"Not necessarily. I didn't suspect her at first, either. Her rigging that robbery and staging that phony attack was very convincing."

"Then how did you know?"

"It all came together the moment I began to question the mummy's authenticity. I realized I had bought into a hoax, that this wasn't about a scientific discovery at all but about professional jealousy and revenge."

"I can understand how much Terese wanted to get even with Talbot," Dawson said. "But how could she murder two people?"

"Two?" McQuede echoed. "What about Roma Fielding?"

"Your aunt just left here a while ago. She called it a miracle. Roma has regained consciousness and is expected to recover."

"That *is* good news." With relief McQuede thought of Roma, of her innocent wanderings, of her helpless animals.

"But Terese is still facing two murder charges." Dawson smiled a little. He rose and laid down a bill for the coffee. "In a way, you could say I'm very fortunate. The arrow you mentioned, I've been able to extract without permanent damage."

McQuede watched him leave, thinking that his advice to the lovelorn wasn't all that successful. Dawson had lost his girl. Ruger had lost his. And what about him? What about Loris Conner? Without bothering to wait for Mom to get over to his table, McQuede walked out of the café.

When he arrived at Loris' house, he found her suitcases packed and sitting by the door. She admitted him with a happy smile. "Now that your name has been cleared of all charges, you'll have no trouble getting reelected."

"But you're not sticking around to vote for me."

After a long silence, Loris said, "Arden has asked me to go to Denver for the next six months to help him with the special exhibit."

McQuede tried to keep his voice level. "So you're going to go."

"I don't know. Jeff, if you really want me to stay . . ."

McQuede wanted more than anything to tell her the

truth—the last thing he wanted was to have her out of his life, even for a matter of months. Yet he knew it was time to follow his own advice. It wasn't about what he wanted anymore, but about what Loris wanted. "I don't see how you can miss out on such a good opportunity."

Loris looked as if a heavy weight had been lifted. "Thanks, Jeff, for being so understanding. After all, it's not for long. We'll keep in touch. I'll be back in no time, and everything will be just the way it was."

He loaded Loris' bags into her car. For a moment they stood awkwardly, as if full of words that would be left unsaid. His girl—Loris. He was so proud of her. He took in every detail—the honey-blond hair, the tailored tan blazer and slacks, which made her look smart and businesslike, yet feminine too. The excited glow in her eyes made them sparkle with green and gold. How he would miss her!

"Call me when you get there."

Loris stepped forward into his arms, and he drew her close. Their lips met, the imminent parting making the kiss bittersweet.

McQuede stood by the squad car and watched her drive away. When she reached the corner, she turned back and waved. He battled an impulse to stop her, yet he knew in his heart that if he wanted any chance with her, he would have to let her go.